A Tale
of
An Arabian
Night

by

VINCENT GILVARRY

A story about love, loss, and courage
In the face of adversity

Published by the Author

Vincent Gilvarry

2024

©

Table of Contents

FOREWORD

A tale of epic proportions unfolds in the fabled city of Aggrabad, nestled in the heart of the Rub al-Khali Desert. The lost city of the Bedouins has been likened to the Atlantis of the Desert, a masterpiece of glistening white limestone, a freshwater oasis shrouded in mystery and romance.

At the heart of this story stands Hakim, the noble Captain of the Guards, who finds himself caught in a web of intrigue and sorcery woven by the tyrannical Sultan Mahmoud ibn Khaleed and the wicked Vizier, Memphalut al Shikari.

The Vizier, a practitioner of the dark arts, rules through fear and cruelty, disposing of his enemies in horrific ways. Hakim must do everything in his power to ensure that this evil man and his plans never come to pass.

CHAPTER 1

Memphalut al Shikari, the Dark Conjurer, stands in the center of his lair, a sanctum of shadows deep beneath the sun-kissed splendor of the fabled city of Aggrabad. The air is thick with the pungent scent of incense that burns upon an altar of dried blood and soot. His long fingers dance through the smoke, weaving spells as ancient as the sands that shield the city from prying eyes.

Inscribed into the stone floor are arcane symbols that pulse with a sickly green light, each a testament to the forbidden knowledge gleaned from scrolls no mortal was meant to read.

Tattered banners bearing sinister symbols hang from the walls, flapping gently as if stirred by the breath of unseen specters. In the middle of this malevolence is a minuscule figure no bigger than a clothes peg, a miniature human being trapped in a crystalline cage.

With a guttural incantation that scrapes at the edge of reality, Memphalut closes his fist, and the sphere implodes, leaving nothing but the fleshy remains of another poor, unfortunate soul. A cruel smile curls the corners of the Vizier's lips, and a bare whisper of satisfaction escapes from his throat.

"Yield to my power," he cries, his voice a low rumble that seems to vibrate through every stone.

He grasps the remains of the man between thumb and forefinger and holds it aloft like a grotesque trinket. With deliberate slowness, he ambles towards a cage in the corner of the room, inside of which is a pair of beady-eyed rats who scurry and squeak, their noses twitching expectantly at the thought of their next meal.

"Feast, my darlings," he says mockingly, the darkness in his soul finding kinship with the vermin that serve him.

He drops the messy mixture into the cage, the rats pounce with voracious glee and devour their first meal of the day. Their master watches, his gaze unblinking and cold, basking in the terror that emanates from a human being who has been reduced to fodder for a few hungry street rats.

"Such is the fate of those who dare to oppose me," Memphalut says, as he savours the sound of bones crunching like a macabre symphony. His enjoyment of suffering is palpable, a dark thrill that courses through his veins and feeds the infernal might that sustains his reign of fear.

As the sound of the crunching ceases, a shadow emerges from the gloom. A sleek raven with feathers as dark as the heart of its master glides through the window and perches upon a jagged ledge that protrudes from the wall.

With eyes that glisten with unnatural understanding, Nightwing surveys the chamber, the arcane symbols etched into stone and the artifacts of forbidden lore that festoon the room.

The raven cocks its head and follows his master's movements with a scrutiny that belies a sentience uncommon to its kind. This is no bird but an extension of the Dark Conjurer's will, a loyal sentinel bestowed with a sliver of his master's malevolent intellect. The creature opens and closes his beak and shares silent secrets that only the Vizier can comprehend.

"Watch well, Nightwing," the Vizier says, his voice carrying the weight of command. "For your eyes shall be mine when I am not present."

Nightwing caws in response, a sound that resonates with obedience and a readiness to serve. The raven flutters its wings, and accepts its charge with an almost human solemnity.

A moment of silent communion is interrupted by the arrival of an ethereal wisp of light coiling through the air like smoke. It materialises into the shape of a scroll sealed with the Sultan's emblem and hovers before the Vizier. He grabs it with a gnarly hand, and the seal dissolves into a puff of brimstone-scented mist.

"Ah, the Sultan calls for me," he says, his thin lips twisting into a smile reflected in his cold, dark eyes. "It seems that my counsel is needed once again."

The Vizier strides across the room and moves with purpose, the hem of his robes following along like the shadow of an eclipse moving across the land. He pauses in front of an ornate mirror, one framed by serpents twisting this way and that in eternal agony.

"Let us see what our dear Sultan requires," he says as he admires his reflection with an arrogance born of countless victories over lesser minds. "No doubt, it's another trivial matter he cannot handle without my guidance."

The mirror responds, not with a reflection but with images of the palace, its white limestone walls shimmering in the relentless sun. Memphalut's gaze penetrates the vision as he dreams of the opulence that awaits him, a stark contrast to the shadows of his abode.

"Come, Nightwing," he says as he strides forward with the confidence of one who knows the extent of his power. "Our presence is required, and we must not keep the Sultan waiting."

The raven takes flight and circles the room before following the Vizier through the grand doors of the Sultan's chamber. They swing open with a silent grace, and welcome the Vizier into a world far removed from the austerity of his lair.

The courtly chamber is a testament to both splendor and excess; vaulted ceilings soar overhead, painted with scenes of conquest and revelry. Sunlight spills through latticed windows, casting a cascade of light that dances upon the gold leaf and jewel-encrusted walls. Emeralds and rubies wink conspiratorially as if recognizing a kindred spirit in the darkness that the Vizier embodies.

The Sultan sits upon his throne, a towering structure of ivory and gold that seems to pierce the very heavens. His figure, clad in sumptuous silks and glinting with precious stones, appears as a mirage of regal opulence amidst the desert of finery.

Yet, even the resplendence of his surroundings pale into insignificance compared to his Vizier's penetrating gaze. The Dark Conjurer's presence seems to leach the colour from the room, leaving nothing but a palette of shadows and whispers.

"Ah, Memphalut, you grace us with your ominous aura," the Sultan remarks, his voice dripping with the honeyed poison of mock welcome.

"Your Majesty, I am but a humble servant to your illustrious will," Memphalut replies, his tone low and resonant as he weaves a spell of deference and flattery.

"Indeed," the Sultan muses as he leans forward, his piercing eyes scanning the Vizier with calculated interest. "And what of the counsel of our advisors? They speak of caution, yet I find their words lack conviction."

"Caution, my Sultan, is the refuge of the weak," Memphalut says as he circles the Sultan like a predator assessing its prey. "Your power is absolute, unchallenged by the whispers of trembling men. It is a truth as radiant as the sun above and as undeniable as the blood that runs through your veins."

"Yet these men of the cloth speak of tradition and the ways of old," the Sultan says, gesturing dismissively. "They would bind me with the chains of antiquity."

"Tradition," the Vizier scoffs, allowing the word to hang in the air like a discarded relic. "A crutch for those who fear progress. Your reign, Oh Lion of Aggrabad, must not be shackled by the outdated musings of religious sycophants. You are the divine wind that shapes the dunes, the falcon that soars above the constraints of narrow minds."

"Indeed," the Sultan replies, a flicker of greed igniting the depths of his hardened soul. "You see clearly, Vizier. Perhaps clearer than most."

"Clarity is but one of my many gifts, my Sultan," he proclaims as he bows deeply, his words laced with the sweet venom of influence. I offer my gifts freely for the glory of your eternal empire."

As the conversation unfolds, the seeds of doubt planted by the Vizier begin to take root in the fertile soil of the Sultan's mind. Each carefully chosen phrase tightens his invisible grip on the ruler's will. With every word, the balance of power imperceptibly shifts, and the tendrils of control stretch further into the heart of Aggrabad's court.

"Permit me, oh mighty Sultan, to suggest a grand opportunity," he says, his voice a sinuous thread weaving through the Sultan's thoughts. "I speak of a splendid festival to celebrate your divine rule and the prosperity of Aggrabad under your guidance."

The Sultan leans forward, intrigued despite himself, his fingers tapping rhythmically against the armrest of his golden throne. "A festival," he muses aloud, his eyes reflecting the flicker of oil lamps that dance like captive djinn.

"Indeed, but this will not be just any celebration," Memphalut says, his gaze never leaving the Sultan's face. "This festival will also mark the unification of religious observance under your exalted leadership, consolidating worship to one temple and one doctrine, yours and yours alone."

A shadow of doubt crosses Sultan's face and a crease forms between his brows. "This is a bold move, Vizier. The clerics hold sway with the people. They might see it as an appropriation of their power."

"Merely a formality," the Vizier says, his lips curling into a sardonic smile. "No, my Sultan, think of it as integration. A single faith under a strong, unifying leader will bring stability to Aggrabad and fortify its foundations against the winds of dissent. And who better to lead than you, the chosen of the gods?"

The Sultan likes that idea and gives it some consideration. "And what of the resistance from the priests?" he asks, his voice betraying the lure of the concept.

"Leave them to me," the Vizier says, his tone imbued with the confidence of a predator focused on its prey. "I shall ensure their cooperation."

The Sultan is impressed. Under the Vizier's masterful persuasion, he is about to chart a very different course. "Make it so," he decrees, his words carrying the weight of destiny.

Night has fallen over Aggrabad by the time the Vizier returns to the chill embrace of his lair. The air is thick with the tang of incense and the sound of rats clawing on stone. He stands amidst his arcane symbols and artifacts, a dark silhouette against the flickering candlelight.

"Masterful," he says to himself, a smirk twisting his parched lips. "As the serpent ensnares the mouse, so too have I bound the Sultan to my will."

He paces slowly, savoring the taste of his triumph, each step resonating through his chamber like a proclamation of his ascendance. His raven caws from its perch, and he regards it with a gleam akin to pride in his otherwise impassive eyes.

"Watch and learn, my pet," he says to Nightwing, his voice low and triumphant. "For this is but the beginning. The clergy will fall, the Sultan shall become my puppet, and Aggrabad shall be molded by my hands."

The raven fluffs its feathers and tilts its head as if to acknowledge the brilliance of its master's schemes. Memphalut laughs quietly, a sound devoid of joy but full of dark promise.

"Let the festival begin," he says as if commanding the very shadows themselves. Like his raven's dark wings, his plans are about to unfurl and enshroud the city in his unyielding grasp. "The dawn of a new era beckons, and none shall stand against the tide of change which I plan to bring forth."

As the night deepens, the Dark Conjurer settles into his throne of gilded bones, surrounded by the malevolent glow of his sorcery, as he plots the next step of his grand design with meticulous care. The game is in motion, and Memphalut al Shikari holds all the pieces.

The stillness of the lair is shattered as the heavy drapery at the door is thrust aside. A figure, robed in black, materializes. This creature is a trusted member of Memphalut's inner circle, and his presence disturbs the Vizier from his contemplative state.

"Master," the servant says, as he bows low to the dark creature seated upon its grotesque throne. The man's voice quivers slightly, betraying the fear that seeps into his mind under the scrutiny of those cold, calculating eyes.

"Speak," the Vizier says, his tone laced with an impatience that can only spell doom for the bearer of ill news.

"I have heard rumors, my lord," the servant says, lifting his gaze just enough to meet the Vizier's dark eyes. "Whispers are being spread among the market folk. They speak of night stalkers, of creatures moving beneath the moon, of whispers that echo your forbidden arts."

Memphalut's hand tightens on the staff adorned by a crystal skull. The shadows in the room seem to deepen and coil around him like serpents ready to strike. "And who," he hisses, "dares to whisper of things they do not understand?"

"That is unknown, master, but the seed of truth within their tales could unravel the threads you have woven so diligently," the subordinate says, his shadow trembling against the stone wall as if fearing his master's wrath.

"Unravel," the Vizier says haughtily. He vaults to his feet, a specter of fury incarnate, his robes billowing as though caught in an unfelt gale. "No tapestry of mine shall be undone by the prattling of commoners!" His voice, now a tempest, echoes off the ancient stones.

"Forgive me, master." The servant bows deeply, his voice a mere wisp. "I came at once to alert you, knowing your wisdom would foresee a path through this...complication."

"A mere complication indeed." The words roll off the Vizier's tongue like bitter venom. He turns away, his mind already weaving more sinister plots. His eyes are aglow as he faces his servant, not with rage but with the fire of dark inspiration.

"Listen well," he says, the calmness in his voice belying the storm within. "You will find these rumor-mongers and use the Nasnas to sniff them out. They excel at sowing discord and will enjoy this task. And once they have been found, silence them. Permanently."

"By your command, it shall be done," the servant says, rising only after his master waves his hand in the air.

"Let no one know of our involvement. If necessary, employ the Falak. Nothing can oppose the ferocity of those serpentine creatures. Their need for destruction is thorough and will obscure our tracks," Memphalut says, his lips curling into a cruel semblance of a smile.

"Understood, master. Your will shall be enacted with discretion," the subordinate assures him as he backs away from the throne and bows before leaving the lair.

Memphalut watches as he retreats and disappears into the gloom. His heart, a barren wasteland of coldness, knows neither concern nor doubt. As the footsteps fade, so too does any trepidation about the preservation of his secrets. The Grand Vizier of Aggrabad, Memphalut al Shikari, does not tolerate fools or threats to his dominion.

The door of his dank lair swings shut with a resounding thud, sealing his commands within its stone embrace. A smug grin slithers across the Vizier's lips, stretching his pallid skin over high cheekbones.

He strolls back to his altar, fingers trailing along the cold limestone surface inscribed with arcane runes. The Grand Vizier revels in the harmonic cadence of control and chaos, the sweet symphony that plays out at the mere thought of his plans unfolding in the shadows of Aggrabad.

"Ah, the intricate dance of power," he says as he picks up an obsidian dagger that glints malevolently in the candlelight. "Every step has been choreographed to perfection."

The satisfaction that blooms in his chest is a dark flower, and as every second passes, he envisions his adversaries falling into ruin. He has set his will upon the world, which will bend or break to accommodate his desires. There is no other outcome that he could possibly entertain.

A sudden flutter of wings attracts his attention. His pet raven, Nightwing, descends from its perch and circles the room before landing gracefully on the table's edge. Its beady eyes hold an intelligence that belies its avian form and cocks its head as if appraising the Vizier's mood.

"Speak, my winged sentinel," Memphalut says, his stern gaze never leaving the bird.

Nightwing caws once, the sound echoing ominously through the chamber, before dropping a small scroll tied with black thread at his master's feet. The Vizier retrieves it, and the paper crackles under his touch as he unravels the scroll to reveal the hastily scrawled message.

"Such defiance," he howls, the words escape like steam from a boiling cauldron. "Hakim dares to refuse my command?"

The parchment that quivers in his hand clearly reveals the defiant stand of the Captain of the Guards. "He refuses to imprison the beggars," the Vizier cries." That is a direct challenge his authority, and his pleasure suddenly turns to poison, a toxic brew of fury and indignation.

"Such impudence cannot go unpunished," he snarls as he crumples the offending message in his fist. The raven caws again, sensing the shift in his master's temper.

"Prepare yourself, Captain," he cries, his eyes ablaze with the promise of retribution. "You have chosen to stand against the tide and will be swept away by its wrath."

He pivots on his heel, his robes swirling around him like a shroud of impending doom. The crystal skull atop his staff seems to leer in agreement, its empty sockets reflecting the unholy fire that burns within the Vizier's blackened soul.

"Summon the Nasnas," he cries to the raven, his voice dripping with malice. "Let them be my instruments of discipline. Hakim will rue the day he dared to defy me."

Nightwing takes flight, a shadow amongst shadows, as Memphalut begins to pace, weaving the web of Hakim's downfall. The Captain of the Guards has become a liability, a stain on the tapestry of his design, and he has to be dealt with.

"Aggrabad will feel my fury," he vows as the words resonate through the lair. "And Hakim Al-Rashid will be the first to feel my vengeance."

CHAPTER 2

The sun hangs high over the city, casting a golden glow upon the limestone walls of Aggrabad, and the Captain of the Guards, Hakim Al-Rashid, strides through the teeming bazaar with the vigilance of an eagle.

He moves with purpose, his sharp green eyes darting from face to face, seeking out the merest hint of malcontent or mischief amongst the people in the marketplace. The weight of the curved scimitar at his hip is a comfort, its presence a reminder of his duty to safeguard the Atlantis of the Desert.

The marketplace is a vibrant tapestry of life woven from the threads of a thousand stories. Each step brings Hakim deeper into the heart of the bazaar, where the air dances with the fragrance of cumin and cardamom.

Merchants clothed in kaftans of amethyst and saffron, advertise their bargains with a lyrical cadence, their voices weaving seamlessly into the hum of activity that buzzes like a hive of desert bees.

"Dates as sweet as the kiss of rain," cries one vendor, his hands gesturing grandly towards a display of glistening fruit. Nearby, another merchant unveils bolts of silk that gleam with the iridescent colors of a peacock's tail, each hue vying for attention under the relentless gaze of the sun.

Hakim pauses, and allows himself to appreciate the craftsmanship of a blade-smith whose stall is adorned with shields and swords that mirror the shimmering oasis at the city's core. The scent of leather and polished metal mingle in the air, tempting even the most frugal passerby with the promise of strength and protection.

A mother haggles fiercely over a carpet that bears the intricate patterns of the ancient Bedouins, her lively negotiation skills drawing a crowd of onlookers. Her young son tugs at the hem of her loose-fitting abaya, his eyes wide with wonder at the kaleidoscope of color that surrounds him. Hakim observes the scene with a soft smile, his stern demeanor momentarily softened by the child's innocence.

As he moves through the bazaar, Hakim's senses remain alert; a captain's instincts are never truly at rest. Yet the marketplace offers no cause for alarm, only the everyday ebb and flow of commerce and community under the vast expanse of the desert sky. In the pulsating heart of Aggrabad, Hakim finds solace amidst his responsibilities, reassured by the enduring rhythm of his beloved city.

As he treads upon the cobblestone path worn smooth by countless others souls, his practiced gaze sweeps over the bazaar. The aroma of spice fills the air with a heady blend of cinnamon and cardamom, but Hakim is attracted by a less vibrant pocket of the marketplace.

Tucked away in a shadowy alcove is a gathering of beggars and cripples who huddle together, their forms draped in tattered cloaks that blend with the dusky tones of the limestone walls. To the untrained eye, they are part of the city's backdrop, as unremarkable as the faded mosaics that adorn the fountains. But to Hakim, whose duty it is to see beyond facades, they are a dissonant note in the market's symphony.

He observes them discreetly, taking note of their number and demeanor. It is not uncommon for the destitute to seek shade from the tyranny of the sun. But there is something about this congregation that whispers of secrets and silent pleas. Rumors waft through the alleyways with tales of beggars who have disappeared around dusk, and it is this thought that nags at the edge of Hakim's mind.

"Many are disappearing without a trace," he says, his voice a low rumble that only the wind can hear. "But what is happening to them?"

Driven by concern and curiosity, he adjusts the scabbard at his hip. He approaches the beggars with the measured confidence of a man who wields authority as deftly as the sword at his side. He knows those who glance surreptitiously in his direction, their eyes flickering with apprehension and something akin to guarded relief.

"Peace be upon you," Hakim says, his tone deliberate, neither threatening nor overly familiar. "I come bearing no ill will."

A few of the beggars nod, their expressions wary but not hostile. One old man whose back is curved like an archer's bow meets Hakim's gaze. Deep within the wells of his eyes is a story etched by time and suffering, a story Hakim feels compelled to understand.

"Captain Al-Rashid," the old man says, his voice gravelly with age. "We are but shadows in the light of Aggrabad's grandeur."

"Shadows have their place," Hakim says as he crouches down to meet the man at eye level. "But even they should not fear being swallowed by darkness. Tell me, have any among you seen or heard anything about your vanishing kin, and by what hand?"

The beggars exchange glances, a silent conversation passing between them before the old man speaks again. "Rumors are as plentiful as sand in the desert, Captain. We hear whispers and feel the unease, but we are without answers. Only the sand dunes know, and they are not forthcoming."

Hakim's jaw is set in determination, the muscles tightening like the strings of an oud. He will find the answer to this mystery somehow or another. With a nod of respect to the beggars, he rises, knowing his investigation has only just begun.

"Keep watch, and should you learn anything, seek me out," he says, his words a solemn vow. "None shall harm you while I draw breath."

With that promise lingering in the air, Hakim steps back into the sunlight. The mystery of the missing beggars is a burden he willingly shoulders. As the bazaar continues to dance around him, Hakim's resolve hardens like steel in a forge. Justice will be served; it's only a matter of time.

The thrum of the bazaar rings in his ears as he strides with purpose, the weight of the beggars' plight rests heavy on his shoulders. But a sudden piercing cry cuts through the din like a scimitar through silk. A raven, its wings outstretched, descends from a cloudless sky and circles above before landing on a nearby pillar.

Hakim's heart quickens. The raven wears an unmistakable silver band around its leg, the mark of the Vizier. He steps forward and extends his arm, allowing the bird to alight upon his leather bracer. With deft fingers, he unrolls the tiny scroll attached to the avian's leg. The message is curt, written in a hand that seems to crawl across the parchment like a nest of scorpions:

"Captain Al-Rashid, attend to me at once."

No signature is needed; the command could only come from one man, Memphalut al Shikari, the Grand Vizier.

Tension coils within Hakim's heart like a caged animal. He cannot ignore this summons without risking the ire of the Dark Conjurer himself, yet his duty to the missing people urges him to remain. Duty wins over curiosity; he cannot forsake his position. With a heavy heart, he releases the bird into the azure sky and sets forth toward the dark domain of the Vizier.

As he approaches the imposing archway leading to Memphalut's quarters, the vibrancy of the bazaar fades into memory. Here, the air is still and heavy, and even it is reluctant to enter the Vizier's domain.

The grandeur of Aggrabad's limestone walls gives way to shadowy corridors where light struggles against the encroaching darkness. Each step echoes ominously, amplified by the silence that clings to the cold stone walls.

The further he ventures, the more the atmosphere thickens with dread. Whispers seem to slither through the dimly lit hallways, a chorus of indistinct voices that could be figments of Hakim's imagination or of distant incantations.

Torches flicker in their sconces, casting ghostly shadows that dance with cruel delight. The air is imbued with foreboding as if the stones hold the memories of dark deeds and whisper to those who will listen.

Hakim's senses are on the alert, his warrior instincts attuned to the unseen dangers that lurk within these oppressive walls. Yet he walks with the unwavering stride of a man who is accustomed to facing peril. His hand rests lightly on the hilt of his sword, but hoping for no cause to use it.

With each step he takes, Hakim is one step closer to the heart of the Vizier's lair, and he can feel the chill of the unknown creeping into his bones. It is here, amidst the whispers and shadows that he will confront the enigmatic will of Memphalut al Shikari and whatever twisted purpose lies behind it.

He knocks on the Vizier's door and enters the chamber, a vast room that seems to swallow up the dim light of the braziers. The walls are adorned with tapestries depicting scenes of conquest and arcane symbols that shimmer with an unsettling energy.

At the far end, upon a throne-like chair wrought from the bones of creatures unknown sits Memphalut al Shikari. His gaunt frame is draped in dark robes that pool around him like oil on water. His eyes, cold and calculating, fix upon Hakim with an intensity that bears down like the desert sun at midday.

"Captain Al-Rashid," the Vizier says, his voice slithering through the air as if it's weaving between shadows. "You are to gather the beggars that cluster like flies at the bazaar's edge. They are a disturbance to the Sultan's peace of mind."

Hakim's heart pounds against his chest plate. He knows of the rumors, the stories about beggars vanishing, never to be seen again. His gaze darts momentarily to the guards who serve the Vizier, their faces obscured by helmets that gleam in the half-light. Their stillness is unnerving, more statue like than man.

Duty wrestles with doubt in Hakim's mind. His loyalty lies with the Sultan, but his paranoia has grown out of proportion, and his rule has become increasingly cruel. And the Vizier? A master spider and a spinner of webs is hiding in the darkness.

To round up the destitute would be to act against those he swore to protect. Yet to defy the Vizier's orders carries a risk that could ripple far beyond this shadowy hall. It's a choice between the lesser of two evils, a decision that weighs heavily on his soul.

"Your will shall be done," Hakim says, his voice betraying none of his inner turmoil. As he inclines his head in deference, a silent vow takes shape in the fortress of his resolve: he will not let injustice go unchallenged. Not while honor still courses through his veins.

The Vizier's thin lips curve into a semblance of a smile, but without any warmth, just the chill of a desert night. "See that it is so, Captain," he replies, as he dismisses Hakim with a languid wave of his hand. "The Sultan's peace must be preserved."

As Hakim turns to leave, the voices in the corridor seem to grow louder, as though the stones are cautioning him of the path that lies ahead.

His boots echo on the cool marble floor and then he pauses, the weight of his duty anchoring him to the spot. The Vizier's decree still hangs in the air, a silent challenge to his honor.

"Forgive my boldness, Grand Vizier," Hakim says, his voice steady despite the tempest brewing in his chest. "May I inquire as to the nature of the crimes these beggars have committed? It is my role to ensure that justice prevails, and that includes understanding why they are to be rounded up."

The Vizier leans forward, steepling his fingers with deliberate calm. "Captain Al-Rashid," he says, his tone laced with condescension, "your duty is to follow orders, not to question them. Their crimes are only of concern to the Sultan, and that should suffice for you."

"Yet if there is no evidence of wrongdoing," Hakim persists, respectful but firm, "are we not then punishing the innocent? Such actions could sow unrest among the people, and it is my duty to protect them."

Memphalut al Shikari's eyes narrow into slits, the darkness of the room gathering around him like a dark cloak. "Unrest," he whispers, his voice now a serpent's hiss. "It is precisely to prevent such chaos that these vermin must be removed. They are a blight upon Aggrabad, a stain upon its beauty. Surely you can see that?"

The tension coils even tighter, each word from the Vizier's lips is a veiled dagger. Hakim holds his ground like a steadfast dune against a relentless wind.

"Beauty, Grand Vizier, is found in the spirit of our city, not merely its appearance. If we are to uphold the true glory of Aggrabad, it must be through compassion and not fear."

A cruel smile twitches at the corner of the Vizier's mouth. "Compassion is a luxury, Captain, and one that we can ill afford in times of peril. You would do well to remember that."

The air grows thick with unspoken threats, and the silence stretches on like the endless desert beyond. Hakim knows the risk of defiance and the possible retribution that might befall him and those that he cares for. Yet his father's teachings resonate within, a beacon of light in the gathering gloom.

"Then, with all respect, Grand Vizier, show me the peril that these people pose," Hakim says, his resolve unwavering. "Grant me the chance to uncover the truth so that I might serve the Sultan, and Aggrabad, with a clear conscience."

For a few moments, the Vizier does nothing but stare, his cold gaze attempting to pierce the armor of Hakim's conviction. Then, with a click of his tongue, he rises from his throne, and the whispering shadows recoil.

"Very well, Captain," he says, his words dripping with venom. "Seek your truth, but heed this warning.

Should you fail to find the justification for their removal, it will be you that answers to the Sultan."

Hakim is all too aware of the look in the Vizier's eyes, but the fire of his courage will not be extinguished by this evil man. "I understand, Grand Vizier, and I accept the consequences of my duty."

The silence in the Vizier's chamber is like the calm before a tempest and fraught with an unseen electricity. Hakim can feel it in his bones, a tension that seems to whisper of dark days ahead.

It would have been easier to bow to the will of Memphalut al Shikari, to bend like a reed in a oasis when the desert winds howl with fury. But Hakim Al-Rashid is no reed; he is as steadfast as the ancient pillars that hold up the grand archways of Aggrabad.

"Without proof of their guilt, I cannot act against the innocent," Hakim says, each word ringing clear and resolute. His stance remains firm and unflinching, even as the shadows around the Vizier seem to coil with malice.

"Your virtue is your weakness, Captain," the Vizier quips, his voice slithering through the room like a Falak on the hunt. "It blinds you to the necessities of power."

"Then let me be blind," Hakim replies, "for I see clearly enough what is just and unjust." His hand rests upon the hilt of his scimitar, an unspoken vow to defend what is right, even if it means standing alone against the might of the Vizier in his dark domain.

A cold laugh escapes the Vizier's lips, a chilling sound that echoes off the high vaulted ceiling. Yet it holds no sway over Hakim's spirit which blazes with the righteousness of his cause.

"Leave now, Captain," the Vizier commands, pointing a dismissive hand towards the towering bronze doors. "But beware of the path you choose. It is lined with thorns that could ensnare even the most valiant hero."

With a curt nod, Hakim turns his back on the Vizier, the weight of confrontation heavy on his mind. Yet it would be lighter than the burden of betrayal if he was to comply with a wrongful order. The ornate doors open before him and groan as if warning him of the perilous road ahead.

As he strides through the corridors, the flickering torchlight casts shadows on the walls, and the air grows cooler with every step that he takes away from the suffocating atmosphere of the Vizier's lair.

Thoughts swirl through Hakim's mind, a maelstrom of worry for the beggars who huddle in secret corners, for his family whose safety he treasures above all, and for the loyalty he owes to the Sultan and the city.

As the last echo of his footsteps fades into the night, Hakim emerges from the darkness of the palace and steps into the silver glow of moonlight. Above him, the stars bear silent witness to the resolve etched upon his face, a promise to himself and to Aggrabad that he will stand against any storm that the Vizier might decide to summon.

And with that, Captain Hakim Al-Rashid sets forth into the shrouded streets. Mystery and danger lurk in the shadows but there is also hope, as bright and as unyielding as the flame in his warrior's heart.

The chill of the night air strikes him with an almost physical force as he strides through Aggrabad's silent alleyways. The moon, a thin crescent, is but a sliver of light in the sky, and casts long, ominous shadows across the undulating sands that encroach upon the city.

Hakim's hand rests on the hilt of his scimitar, its weight a reassuring promise of protection and power. With every step he takes, the confrontation with the Grand Vizier replays in his mind like a haunting melody whistling through the hollow horns of a Shadhavar.

The Vizier's veiled threats echo in his ears, and Hakim is all too conscious of the undercurrents of danger that lap at the shores of the oasis city. It seems as if the very air of Aggrabad has grown thick with the scent of an impending storm, a confrontation that will test the mettle of even the most seasoned warriors.

He passes through a stone archway, its intricate carvings dulled by the passage of time and pauses. His green eyes, sharp, even in the dim light, scans the emptiness before him.

The bazaar, once teeming with life, now lies deserted; the vibrant tapestries and stalls of the merchants stand as mute sentinels to the silence. The dichotomy between day and night in Aggrabad is stark, and it serves as a reminder that darkness holds its own secrets—secrets that might soon be dragged into the unforgiving light of day.

His thoughts return to the missing beggars, their presence dismissed by most but never overlooked by a captain who has sworn to safeguard all citizens.

Hakim knows that whatever poison lurks behind this mystery, whether man or myth, it will not remain hidden for long. If the Vizier seeks to use these people for some nefarious purpose, then it is his duty to unravel the truth, regardless of the political mire that awaits.

As Captain of the Guards, Hakim al Raschid has walked the line between law and order countless times but never has the balance felt so precarious. The Vizier's command was clear, yet Hakim's heart, a compass guided by justice, refuses to lead him down a path marred by tyranny and oppression.

He turns his gaze toward the stars, seeking the wisdom of his ancestors who once navigated these very streets. Their legacy is one of honor and valor, and Hakim will not allow the darkness of one man's ambition to sully their memory.

Determined footsteps carry him away from the heart of Aggrabad, where the limestone buildings gleam like bones in the moonlight. He moves towards the outskirts, where the desert reclaims its dominion and where answers lie buried beneath the ever-shifting dunes.

As the first hint of dawn tinges the horizon with the faintest blush, Hakim Al-Rashid knows that the coming day will bring more than the sun's warmth; it will ignite the flames of conflict.

The stage is set, and even though the players may be unwilling, they are about to act out a drama that has been foretold, both by whispered prophecies and the alignment of celestial bodies.

A new chapter awaits, the pages are blank, and the ink has not yet been spilled. But when it is written, it will tell the tale of a captain's courage, a city's fate, and the unyielding spirit of a man who stood as the last bastion against the creeping shadow of a Vizier's dark ambition.

CHAPTER 3

It is the first day of the seventh month and a day of portentous celebrations as members of the court dressed in sumptuous robes congregate in front of an imposing edifice that overlooks an oasis on the outskirts of Aggrabad.

The sun is a golden orb suspended in a pristine azure sky, its rays caressing the limestone walls of the palace which shimmers like a mirage in the heart of Aggrabad. A grand ceremony is about to unfold, and the Sultan's entourage wait patiently, protected from the heat by huge silken umbrellas.

Sultan Mahmoud ibn Khaleed stands regally at the forefront, his opulent robes a cascade of gold and jewels that reflect his immense wealth and power. The air is heavy with the scent of exotic spices and blooming flowers, and the atmosphere is charged with anticipation.

In stark contrast to the resplendence that surrounds him, the Iman, cloaked in austere garb, observes the scene with a furrowed brow. His eyes, dark wells of consternation, follow the Sultan's every move with an intensity that belies his inner turmoil.

The ceremony begins, and the Sultan raises his arms and invokes the favor of deities that lie beyond the domain of traditional belief, a clear affront to the faith he once professed.

The Iman's fingers twitch nervously at his side as he watches the Sultan bow before a grand altar dedicated to foreign entities. A cold knot tightens in his stomach, for it is not just any god to whom the Sultan pays homage, but the dreaded Djinn, capricious and powerful genies. Such worship threatens the very fabric of their world, yet none dare to challenge the tyrant for fear of his cunning intellect and iron-fisted rule.

His lips pressed thin, the Iman leers at the Sultan, conscious of the paranoia etched into his face and the piercing eyes that miss nothing. No one else seems to notice the religious leader's silent disapproval, and if they do, they mask it beneath layers of feigned adoration for their ruler. The Sultan's voice echoes across the gathering, commanding and condescending, as he continues to extol the virtues of his newfound allies in the spiritual realm.

"Behold the might of Aggrabad," he declares, "blessed by powers greater than the confines of our ancestors' narrow vision!"

The Iman tenses, his heart, a battleground of faith and fear. To speak out against the Sultan is to invite death, yet to remain silent is to condone sacrilege. He glances around at the people in the crowd: merchants, soldiers, citizens, all united under the Sultan's reign yet divided in their hearts between loyalty and the sound of their conscience.

A sudden tremor beneath the Iman's feet breaks his reverie. It's but a subtle quiver and easily dismissed amidst the revelry. Yet, it speaks volumes to the religious leader who understands the language of divine discontent. His troubled gaze lingers on the Sultan, who is oblivious to the undercurrents of dissent and the subtle warning offered by the earth itself.

As the ceremony reaches its zenith, the Iman withdraws into the shadows, a solitary figure grappling with the weight of his convictions against the backdrop of a city blinded by splendor and teetering on the edge of an unseen peril.

His chest heaves with a tumultuous breath as a celestial command erupts from the earth and courses through his veins like liquid fire. His eyes, once clouded with doubt, now shine with an unyielding clarity, a beacon amidst the sea of opulence and sacrilege. He raises his hands to the sky, and with palms open, he beseeches the heavens in a voice laced with the fervor of his faith.

"O Allah, Most Merciful, Most Just," the Iman intones, his voice resounding above the din of celebration, "witness the transgressions of Sultan Mahmoud ibn Khaleed, and punish this heathen. He has forsaken your name and chooses to worship idols dedicated to the dreaded Djinn. Lead your flock back into the light of Your grace."

The crowd falls into stunned silence, the revelry halted by the raw power in the Iman's cry. Wide-eyed and mouths agape, they turn from the spectacle of the Sultan's grandeur to the solitary figure challenging the very foundation of their world.

Fear ripples through their hearts, a wave, not of awe but of trepidation. Their beliefs have been shaken by the Iman's proclamation. Whispers spread like wildfire, the words 'blasphemy' and 'divine retribution' are traded between lips that had, only moments before, sang the praises of their ruler.

The Sultan's loyal guards, clad in their gleaming armour, exchange uncertain glances. Their hands hover over scimitars, uncertain as to whether they should quell this burst of divine passion or let the judgment of a higher power unfold. Cloaked figures in the crowd clutch prayer beads, their silent recitations joining the Iman's plea for heavenly intervention.

Fear supplants uncertainty, as the visage of the Iman, illuminated by an otherworldly conviction is etched into the collective minds of the citizens of Aggrabad. A city built upon the sands of tradition and faith finds itself at a crossroads; its destiny hangs on the precipice of the divine and the profane.

Beneath the splendor of Aggrabad, where the roots of ancient palms reach deep into the earth's embrace, an underground chamber echoes with a sound that has no place in the realm of the living. It is as if the very stones are groaning under the weight of centuries. This low rumble seems to speak of long-forgotten curses and the wrath of gods usurped by mortal vanity.

In the shadows, where the lavish tapestries of the palace above do not cast their opulence, the air grows thick with the scent of damp earth, and something more sinister, an expectancy that claws at the fringes of reality.

And then, the walls vibrate imperceptibly, as though resonating with the heartbeat of a slumbering giant. A tremor follows and a vast plume of sand rains down over the city and covers everything in a fine layer of dust.

Unaware of the dark omens unfurling beneath his gilded feet, the Sultan presides over a grand ceremony with the self-assured poise of one who believes himself to be the master of all that he surveys.

Draped in robes that shimmer like the desert sun, his presence commands attention, and his voice, rich with the timbre of absolute power, rises above the hushed murmurs of the conflicted crowd.

"Behold the wonders that my reign has wrought," he proclaims as he sweeps his arms wide to encompass the grandeur of his palace, the testament to his might. "Let the heavens themselves gaze down in envy, for they shall find no equal to the magnificence of Aggrabad."

The looks on the faces of the people is a mosaic of reverence and doubt, but they dare not challenge the Sultan's authority. Even as they bow their heads, the ground beneath them whispers of turmoil, its voice unheard amidst the cacophony of celebration and the Sultan's towering pride.

The Sultan's piercing eyes reflect the evening light like dark stars, and he smiles, a cruel twist of lips that know neither mercy nor humility. "I am the chosen of the gods," he declares, his voice cutting through the air like a scimitar unsheathed. "My will is the divine architect of our destiny."

The ominous sound from the chamber below rumbles again, a discordant symphony heralding a fate that no man can escape, not even a Sultan cloaked in arrogance. And yet, as the very earth begins to sing its portentous lullaby, the Sultan remains ensconced in his delusions of grandeur, blind to the peril that is stirring just beneath the sands of his beloved Aggrabad.

The earth trembles, a subtle shiver at first, like the whisper of sand slipping through an hourglass. The murmur of the assembled crowd falters, and the Sultan pauses mid-sentence, his eyes narrowing not in concern but irritation. As he stands before his gleaming limestone palace, the trembling grows more insistent, commanding the attention of all.

"Steady yourselves," he cries, mistaking the unease of his subjects for weakness. His voice echoes off the grand columns, striving to quell the nascent fear that dances across the faces of courtiers and commoners alike.

But the ground finds its voice, a deep and resonant growl that rises from the very bowels of Aggrabad. The marble slabs beneath their feet shift, clattering against each other with a sound like bones rattling in the throes of a plague.

Women clutch at children; men reach for their swords, but nothing can protect them against this unseen foe. The air is filled with the scent of dust and panic as tapestries sway and palm fronds shudder under the strain of an invisible beast.

"Peace," the Sultan commands, his opulent robes undisturbed by the chaos that unfurls around him. "It is but a tremor, a petty tantrum of the earth." His laugh is meant to be a balm but it sounds hollow against the cacophony of the rising alarm.

As the shaking intensifies, jewel-encrusted goblets clink melodically against platters heavy with dates and figs, spilling their riches unheeded onto the ground. The Sultan's guards struggle to maintain their dignified formation; their armor clinks discordantly as they fight to keep balance amidst the undulating waves of stone and sand.

"Stand firm," the Sultan cries, as he raises his arms as if to hold the very sky aloft. His eyes blaze, reflecting the torchlight that flickers desperately against the encroaching darkness. But his words are swallowed by a roar that erupts from the earth, and it is not a mere tremor but a mighty bellow of unrest.

"See how it ceases at my command," the Sultan boasts moments before a violent jolt sends him staggering back a step, and briefly shatters his control. The sycophants at his side rush to steady their ruler, their own terror barely concealed beneath layers of obsequious concern.

Yet still, the Sultan's pride holds sway over reason, and he sneers at the trembling ground, dismissing the portent of doom that rumbles beneath the city he rules with such merciless certainty. His refusal to acknowledge the danger is as immovable as the ancient stones of Aggrabad itself, even as the surrounding stone walls threaten to come crashing down around him.

The splendor of Aggrabad is an empire on the brink, and the Iman watches in horror as the Sultan's hollow laughter rebounds against the discord of a protesting earth. His aged hands are clasped so tightly that the Imam's knuckles shine pale against his sunburnt skin.

"O Protector," he whispers under his breath, his voice a mere thread amidst the chaos, "guide my steps to shield the innocent."

His gaze, darkened with sorrow never leaves the Sultan's face. Mahmoud still stands resplendent and oblivious upon the dais, a figure of gold and arrogance. But the Iman sees through his façade. He sees a man who has lost his way, blinded by power and deaf to the cries of his people.

The ground heaves again and screams fill the air. The Iman moves, not towards safety, but closer to the turmoil. His presence is a balm to the panicked masses, his very being an unwavering pillar amidst the sea of uncertainty. They look to him, eyes wide with fear, seeking solace, and he offers it freely, for his faith is their fortress.

"Stand true, children of Aggrabad," he cries, his voice gaining strength. "Let your hearts not be troubled by one man's folly!"

It is then that the very sands of time stir beneath the ground, and the scene becomes a place of chaos where light dare not linger.

Deep beneath the city's heart, an underground chamber thrums, sounding more ancient than the desert itself. It is a voice that issues from the belly of the earth, a prelude to a fury long held at bay.

In that shadowed realm, where no opulent tapestry can hide the raw face of stone, the walls begin to betray the facade of invincibility. Cracks appear in the limestone walls, creeping like sinister veins. Each new fissure is a silent scream in the darkness, a herald of the reckoning that is to come.

Dust dances in the scant rays of light that penetrate this subterranean space, each particle aglow with foreboding. The sound swells, a crescendo of dread until the very air vibrates with intensity. Stones dislodge from their ancient resting places and tumble to the ground with muted thuds, hushed before the impending doom.

No human eye can behold the omens within these depths, yet they speak in a language that transcends sight, a language of destruction soon to be felt by all.

The earth beneath the white stone pavers of Aggrabad's grand plaza trembles with a newfound wrath, sending shockwaves through the soles of every reveler's feet. What had begun as mere whispers beneath the ground erupts into a chorus of tremors that cannot be ignored. The Sultan's grand ceremony, once awash with the fragrance of exotic spices and the gentle sound of flowing water is inundated with a symphony of terror.

"It's an earthquake," someone cries out, their voice piercing the cacophony like a blade through silk.

A ripple of panic surges through the crowd as the realization strikes them all at once. Men and women dressed in ornate clothes push against each other; their cries mingle with the clatter of ceremonial ornaments crashing to the ground. Children wail, ensnared in the sea of legs scrambling for safety, while elders stumble, their pleas drowned by the clamor.

At the epicenter of it all stands the Sultan, his towering figure swaying unsteadily as the earth shakes beneath him. His opulent robes, glimmering like the desert sun only moments before, seem dim in the shadow of impending doom. His piercing eyes, accustomed to instilling fear, now flicker with the reflection of a man witnessing the end of his empire.

"Silence! Stand your ground," he bellows over the tumult, but his commanding tone falters against the primal dread that grips his subjects.

The guards, clad in shimmering chainmail, clutch at their curved scimitars, their usual stoicism giving way to unease. They look to their Sultan for guidance yet find him as mortal as they are, his face etched with lines of concern that betray his inner turmoil.

"Maintain order," the Sultan cries, but his voice lacks its usual conviction. "This is but a trifling disturbance."

But the earth vehemently disagrees and shakes ever more violently, like an ancient beast awakening from its slumber. Cracks appear in the plaza, and stones are jostled loose from the palace walls. The splendor of Aggrabad crumbles bit by bit, its glory falling as easily as dust from a neglected windowsill.

The Sultan's heart pounds against his ribcage, a drumbeat of fear that mirrors the surrounding chaos. He has ruled with an iron fist, believing himself to be invulnerable, a deity among men. Yet, as the ground roils and his city descends into bedlam, the stark revelation claws at him—there are powers beyond his control, and forces that even a Sultan cannot command.

"Protect me!" he cries, finally succumbing to the terror that enslaves his people.

His guards form a hasty circle around their master, swords drawn as if steel could fend off nature's wrath. The populace scatter. Some disappear into alleyways, others race for the safety of palace, their faces masking their desperation.

Above them, the azure sky remains unperturbed, an indifferent witness to the catastrophe unfolding below. As the earth continues to rebel, it becomes clear that the Sultan's fear is not a result of the trembling ground alone. It is the realization that his rule, his very legacy, might be swallowed whole by the sands from which it rose.

The air is thick with dust and dread, and the once-magnificent spires of Aggrabad quiver like reeds in the wind. Sultan Mahmoud ibn Khaleed, his opulent robes now smeared with the grime of his falling city, watches in stunned silence as the fractures in the earth spread like a plague, each new chasm a testament to his hubris.

"Your Majesty, we must leave," one of his guards cries, his voice straining over the cacophony of destruction.

The Sultan's piercing eyes, which have so often instilled fear, flicker with uncertainty. He takes an unsteady step backwards, the ground beneath him betraying his every move. His palace, a symbol of his might, groans ominously. Its limestone façade no longer sparkles in the desert sun, dulled by an impending doom.

"Where will we go?" he cries. The words are but a whisper, drowned out by his crumbling empire.

From the corner of his eye, he sees a young child separated from her mother, her cries piercing the tumult. It's a stark reminder that his people are not mere chess pieces in his grand design, they are flesh and blood, their lives interwoven with the fate of Aggrabad itself.

"Save them," he cries, his voice regaining some of its former authority, but it wavers, betraying his inner turmoil.

As the guards hasten to aid the fleeing citizens, the Sultan is conscious of a chilling isolation that settles upon his shoulders. No longer is he surrounded by sycophants or subjects; it's just him and the vast, indifferent desert sky.

The ground lurches violently and throws him to his knees. A great roar fills the air, louder than that of any beast, any war drum, any tempest he has ever known. It is as if the very bowels of the earth seek vengeance for the sacrilege wrought upon it.

In the distance, a shadow looms, a colossal cloud of sand and debris that barrels it way toward the heart of Aggrabad. Is this the divine retribution the Iman had called for? Is this the end of everything he has built?

As a wall of destruction bears down upon them, the Sultan's figure appears trivial against the vastness, his silhouette enveloped by the wrath of the desert. Aggrabad's fate hangs by a thread; its legacy is on the brink of being erased by the sands that once cradled it to greatness.

CHAPTER 4

On the day before everything changed, a catastrophe was predicted by the seeress, Zarqa Al-Yamana. As to her age, no one knows but she is a commanding presence and well respected. Whenever Zarqa is about to deliver a proclamation, the hustle and bustle in the marketplace dies away and barely a noise can be heard.

She usually sits in a state of mystical union and reaches into the silence, her eyes taking on an ethereal glow like deep pools of wisdom, and time itself seems to slow when she starts to speak.

"Children of the sands, heed my words," she had said, her voice resonating with an unsettling, out-of-this-world timbre. "The tapestry of fate is unfurling in my mind and is about to reveal its ominous weave."

"Destruction will come, and with it a cleansing fire from the hand of God to claim this Atlantis of the Desert."

A collective shiver coursed through the crowd as Zarqa spoke. Disbelief struck first, etching lines of confusion on weathered faces. Some people scoffed, their chuckles hollow in the still air. Others yet again exchanged skeptical glances, seeking reassurance in shared doubt. But Zarqa's gaze was unwavering, and disbelief slowly turned to unease.

"Aggrabad shall weep tears of sand," she cried, her voice imbued with a foreboding power, "and the City of the Bedouins will be lost to all time, reclaimed by the dunes from whence it sprang."

Murmurs rippled through the assembled crowd like a wind through desert reeds as the prophecy took root in their hearts. Men sought comfort in the feel of leather-bound swords, while mothers drew their children closer and wrapped them in the folds of their garments.

The tension in the crowd became tighter, like a coiled serpent ready to strike. Fear was now a palpable specter as it crept along the palm-lined streets and whispered of the destiny of this beautiful city.

As the last echoes of Zarqa's chilling proclamation faded into the air, a heavy silence settled over the city. It was the calm before a storm, laden with the weight of uncertainty and the dread of what might come to pass.

Aggrabad, the jewel of the Rub al-Khali Desert, stood on the precipice of an unknown fate, its people bound by a prophecy that could spell the end of everything they knew and loved.

But the whispers of doom reached beyond the palace walls, and finally made their way to the throne room itself. To quell the unease, the Sultan, draped in opulent robes decided to intervene and make an appearance on the royal balcony.

"That prophecy shall not come to pass," he cried, in an attempt to silence the fears of those who had momentarily forgotten that he was the power in this land and not a seeress of ill repute.

"Let not your hearts be troubled by the ravings of a soothsayer," he said, the scorn in his tone turning each word into a barbed dismissal.

"I am the Sultan Mahmoud ibn Khaleed, chosen by the divine to lead you, and it is under my protection that Aggrabad shall stand unblemished."

He raises his arms in an attempt to encompass the splendor of the city. "No harm shall ever befall this place of prosperity, this oasis of our people."

A few hesitant cheers rose from the throng, but they were quickly stifled by a lingering and now well established dread. But the Sultan's arrogance remained undiminished. He stood in the blazing Sun as if he was its equal, a god amongst mortals who would never bow before the whims of fate.

But there were other eyes watching this pallid performance. Hidden in the shadows of a covered alcove, away from the scorching heat and prying eyes,

Memphalut al Shikari—the Dark Conjurer—was observing that spectacle with a different kind of hunger.

A thin, sinister smile crept across his gaunt cheeks and the light of mischief danced in his cold eyes. From his clandestine perch, he observed the Sultan and the subtle cracks that were forming in the veneer of his soul.

"Ah, dear Sultan," he said to himself, his low, menacing voice barely more than a whisper yet filled with dark delight. "How little you understand the forces you mock."

With every word of false assurance spoken by the Sultan, the Vizier's grin widened. The chaos promised by Zarqa Al-Yamana was a symphony to his ears, and he longed to conduct its progress with the grace of a maestro.

In the mayhem to come, he saw not destruction but an opportunity for power and control that only one such as he, who is versed in the arcane, can navigate.

The Vizier's gaze scanned the sea of anxious faces, and savoured the taste of fear like a fine wine. His anticipation for the disorder that would soon engulf the city shone with a fervor that could only rival the desert sun itself. For where others saw only peril, Memphalut al Shikari saw the potential to harness this storm and rise amidst the sands reshaped by prophecy.

The eyes of the Captain of the Guards, Hakim Al-Rashid are also scanning a sea of faces awash with dread. His jaw is clenched as if to fortify his resolve against the tide of worry that threatens to breach the city walls.

The seer's words hung heavy in the air, a portent that seemed all too real within these shimmering limestone walls. He could feel the weight of his father's legacy upon his broad shoulders, the responsibility woven into his very being to shield the city from harm.

A slight and almost imperceptible gesture passed between Hakim and his men. No words were needed. Their glances spoke of a silent pact to stand guard over Aggrabad, come what may.

The pulse of the city suddenly quickened, and then, without warning, it started. The wind swept in from the desert like an avenging spirit, relentless and wild. And Hakim's cloak was torn asunder as he braced against the burgeoning gale.

This once tranquil oasis was in danger, its exotic spices and desert flowers now overshadowed by the howl of the tempest. Sand snaked its way through the streets in undulating waves, a relentless tide that sought to reclaim the city for the desolate embrace of the desert.

Palm trees, those steadfast sentinels of Aggrabad, bowed beneath the might of the storm, their fronds flickered like the flames of a thousand candles in a furious dance. Citizens staggered, their hands covering their eyes, seeking shelter from the desert's abrasive caress. Their cries were swallowed by the roar that filled the air, a cacophony of sound that seemed to echo Zarqa's dire prophecy.

For seven days and seven nights, the tempest raged. It clawed at the city's grandeur and etched its fury into the very stones that have stood for ages. Hakim moved among the people, a constant presence amidst the chaos. When he could be heard above the storm, his voice was a bastion of command, urging calm and offering guidance in the face of nature's wrath.

The people did their best to endure the onslaught, and Hakim remained vigilant, his every sinew tense against the barrage. His presence was a banner in the tempest, his olive skin gritted with sand, yet his piercing gaze never wavered.

In this battle against the elements, the Captain of the Guards would not yield. His devotion to Aggrabad was as unassailable as the ancient mysteries that shroud her past, a commitment carved deep into his soul, as enduring as the desert itself.

The sandstorm threatened to rip the very stars from the sky, and with each new gust, the terror mounted. The broad thoroughfares, once aglow with lanterns, now lay in darkness, littered with the wreckage of market stalls. Carpets that had once adorned the bazaar like petals in a desert bloom were caught in the maelstrom. The air, thick with dust and dread, carried the sound of timber splintering and stone grinding against stone.

Hakim Al-Rashid watched as his beloved city plunged into pandemonium. Women clutched their children, their faces etched with frantic desperation, as they raced toward any semblance of refuge.

Men fought against the might of the tempest, their shouts barely audible over the howling winds. The aged and infirm stumbled, their pleas for mercy lost in the cacophony. Fear ruled their hearts, and chaos reigned supreme as the prophecy unfolded before their eyes.

"Form lines and secure those canopies," Hakim had cried, his voice cutting through the tumult, raw and forceful. He stood firm, a sentinel amidst the sandstorm's rage, his guards rallying to his side. With practiced efficiency, they worked to tether what remained of the marketplace and provide some shelter from the relentless barrage of sand.

"Check every home. Leave no one behind," he cried as he pointed toward the residential quarters, beneath which lay the remains of barely visible limestone dwellings. His men did his bidding. their expressions grim but resolute as they dispatched squads throughout the beleaguered city.

"Sir, the eastern wall is about to crumble," said a worried guard, his silhouette ghostly in the swirling sand.

"Shore it up. Use whatever you can, barrels and crates," Hakim said as he hastened towards the endangered structure. His broad shoulders bore the brunt of the wind's fury as he stacked heavy objects against the weakening barrier.

Through the chaos, he moved with purpose, his presence a beacon of hope in the heart of the storm. Each command he issued was obeyed without hesitation, and each action was taken with the fierce determination to protect all that he held dear. The lives of the people hung by a thread, and he would be damned if he would let it disappear on his watch.

"Captain, there are children trapped in that house over there," a young guard cried as he pointed toward a dwelling that had all but collapsed under the weight of the sand.

Without thinking, Hakim raced over to see what he could do, his men at his heels. Together, they braved the biting sand, their hands working with desperate speed to clear debris and rescue terrified souls.

"Stay close," Hakim cried to the huddled figures as he led them to safety, his arms shielding the smallest from the cruel winds. The fear in their eyes mirrored the uncertainty of the night, but in Hakim's steady grip, they found solace.

Even as the world was falling to pieces around them, Hakim Al-Rashid didn't falter. Every ounce of his being was devoted to Aggrabad. The winds sought to erase the city from memory, but he would not allow it to end there, not on this night and not as long as he drew breath.

His boots sank into the sand and his cloak was flapping violently in the relentless wind. He battled the onslaught, and as the chaos before him increased, it threatened to overwhelm Aggrabad and the steadfast resolve in his chest.

"Captain, this is impossible," one of his guards cried over the roar of the storm. For a fleeting moment, doubt, as insidious as the sand seeping into every crevice crept into Hakim's heart.

"Am I capable of doing this?" he wondered. The question clawed at his mind and burrowed deep into his consciousness. Can one man stand against the fury of the heavens?" His father's legacy weighed on his mind, the memory of the elder al-Rashid's unwavering strength was a stark contrast to the tremor Hakim felt in his bones.

"Focus, Hakim," he chastised himself. "Your city needs you." With an effort that seemed herculean amidst the swirling tempest, Hakim pushed his doubts aside and summoned the image of his people, all of whom were frightened but looked to him for guidance. It was for them that he had to be strong; it was for them that he had to find a way.

Gathering his courage against the gale, Hakim made for the council chambers where the religious leaders were hiding away. Robed in their faith, and cloaked in wisdom, they were huddled in urgent debate. The chamber buzzed with tension; their fear was palpable, each one glancing to the door where nature's wrath painted a grim picture.

"We must be strong," Hakim cried, his voice cutting through the clamor and silencing the room. Respectful eyes turned to him, seeking direction from the Captain of the Guards. "We cannot allow our fears to divide us when unity is our greatest defense."

"Captain Al-Rashid speaks truly," said the Grand Imam, his aged face lined with concern. "But how can we devise a plan when the Sultan scoffs at the threat? He simply ignored the warnings of Zarqa Al-Yamana."

"Prophecy or not," Hakim said firmly, "we have a city to protect. If we are to weather this storm, we must act now, with or without the Sultan's assistance."

The room erupted into fervent discussion as Hakim laid out a few practical measures such as securing buildings, rationing supplies, and establishing shelters. Each suggestion was met with nods or shakes of the head, their traditional beliefs lost on the urgency of the situation.

"Let us pray, yes," Hakim said, "but let us also work together. The gods favor those who help themselves."

"Then we shall support you, Captain," said a venerated elder, her voice rising above the discord. "It is clear that your heart beats in tandem with Aggrabad's pulse. Lead us through this trial."

As plans were made and roles assigned, the weight of responsibility coalesced into action. The doubt that had flickered in Hakim's mind was extinguished, only to be replaced by the flames of determination. He stood at the center of a city besieged, not yet broken, a beacon of hope and courage.

"Prepare yourselves," he said with newfound conviction. "For we shall endure this calamity. We shall emerge from it stronger than ever before."

Beneath the wrathful sky, the Captain led his guards into the heart of the tempest. Sand and wind clawed at their cloaks, enshrouding them in a tumultuous dance of desert fury. The city of Aggrabad, once a paragon of secluded beauty, now writhed under the siege of nature's unrelenting assault.

"Stay close," Hakim cried, his voice barely audible over the howling gale that sought to sweep them off their feet. His piercing green eyes, shielded by the hand that guarded his face, scanned the chaos for signs of life amidst the crumbling remains of the city.

One by one, they encountered victims of the tempest. A woman clutching her wailing child, trapped beneath a fallen palm. With a herculean effort, Hakim and his men lifted the tree and freed them. A young man, his leg pinned under the rubble of what was once his home, cried until they dug him out and placed him on an improvised stretcher.

"Courage, friends. We must leave no soul behind." Hakim's words were as much a command to his men as they were a promise to the people they had yet to save.

Each rescue fuelled their resolve, but the storm showed no mercy. It raged on, turning day into night with relentless abandon, and even obscured the Sun in the sky above. Yet Hakim, his broad shoulders bearing the weight of every life he saved, refused to succumb to fear or despair.

As they moved through the winding streets, a cry for help pierced the cacophony. They came upon a shattered dome, the jewel of the marketplace now a tomb of debris. Desperate sobs echoed from within the ruins, where a group of merchants had sought refuge only to become prisoners of fate.

"Form a chain," Hakim cried as he worked alongside his men and removed the heavy stones. Each moment was a battle against time and the elements, their faces stung by the relentless onslaught of sand.

"Captain, the structure is unstable," said one of the guards as he eyed the precarious remnants of the dome which threatened to collapse even further.

"We have no choice. Those people are relying on us," Hakim said, the steely edge in his voice betraying no hint of the fear that gripped his heart. "On my count, now everyone, pull."

With a collective heave, they dislodged a large slab and revealed a narrow breach. The eyes of the trapped merchants were filled with both terror and relief. Hakim pulled them out one by one, their expressions a mixture of gratitude and disbelief.

"Quickly, find some shelter," Hakim said as he ushered them toward safety. The last of the survivors were freed, and then, the ground began to rumble.

"Find shelter somewhere else," he roared as the walls of the dome groaned ominously.

Hakim and his men dived for cover as the structure gave one final, mournful sigh before succumbing to the storm's wrath, and collapsed in a cloud of dust and despair. In the silence that folllowed, Hakim's thoughts were racing. How many more will have to suffer this fate? Can they reach them all in time?

Determination was etched into his face. There was no room for doubt, not when lives hung in the balance. "We need more men to help us," he said. "This night is far from over."

And with the fate of Aggrabad teetering on the edge of ruin, Hakim Al-Rashid, the Captain of the Guards, steeled himself for the trials that were yet to come.

CHAPTER 5

Long before this day had ever dawned, the streets of Aggrabad had thrummed with laughter whenever a little bird darted through the crowd. It was the nimble form of Hakim's beloved friend, Zenobia, who entertained the crowds by flying around the marketplace. Her abilities were a gift from an old sorcerer, but for a time, she had come to the attention of the Vizier, the man who sought to control this great city.

Those gifts allowed her to assume the form of a bird, and she loved to follow Hakim around the city. The flutter of her wings was a clear signal that Zenobia had transformed her body yet again and was now no bigger than a sparrow. She usually took to the air, zipping between swaying palm fronds and over the tapestries that adorned the open-air stalls.

The faces of the people, particularly the children, came alive with curiosity and wonder whenever she was around. They marvelled at the magic creature that graced their day-to-day struggles.

"Zenobia," the children would call out in unison. They loved the little bird that was always flying this way and that. And to preserve the magic of the experience, she would settle on Hakim's turban, like a queen bestowing favours upon her subjects.

Sensing their awe and admiration, she would transform from one thing to another and then return to her human form with a graceful flourish that left the children gasping in amazement.

"Tell us a story, Zenobia," they would cry. "Sing to us," they would plead, their eager little faces always desperate for more.

With a nod from Hakim, Zenobia would weave tales of distant lands and skies uncharted, her voice rising and falling like the ebb and flow of the desert winds. Her songs spun stories of heroism and hope, each note carrying the promise of escapades far beyond the confines of their city walls.

On occasions like this, Hakim was always on the lookout for the Vizier's guards, a silent guardian for the enchantress as she held court. And in this hidden corner of a desert paradise, a different kind of light shone, one that glowed from within the hearts of the children who were entranced by Zenobia's words and songs.

Their laughter rose in a sweet crescendo, and mingled with the dust motes dancing in the sunlight. Zenobia's voice, as melodious as the songbirds that she so often emulated, spun a tapestry of fairytales that held her young listeners spellbound.

Her tales were a balm to their roughened spirits, and painted pictures of lush gardens and heroic deeds, each narrative a delicate escape from the harshness of their daily lives.

Hakim always stood back with his arms crossed over his chest, watching the scene with a tender gaze. In moments like these, Zenobia transformed before his eyes, not just through some mystic power, but through the sheer force of her compassion.

She was a beacon in a world too often shrouded in shadow, and his heart swelled with an emotion far more profound than mere admiration. It was love, fierce, and as unwavering as the desert sun.

Moments like these reminded him of why they fought so fiercely, not only for their beloved city but also for the dreams and laughter of those who called it home.

After the stories had wound down and the final threads of enchantment settled over the children's dream-laden eyes, she turned to the man she loved, her eyes alight with the fading echoes of her tales.

"Come, let us find solace under the sky's embrace before night falls," he said as she took her arm with a promise of the quietude that only they could share.

Hand in hand, they slipped away from the alcove, leaving behind the whispers of gratitude and wonder. The streets of Aggrabad were usually empty as the city prepared for evening prayers, allowing them to pass unnoticed to the outskirts where the heartbeat of the desert was strongest.

They often found refuge on the slope of a dune, where the mighty Rub al-Khali stretched out before them like a sea of tranquility. Here, the noise of the city faded into a distant memory, replaced by the sound of rustling sand and their own steady breath.

Seated side-by-side, hands clasped as if nothing could pry them apart, they bore witness to the celestial spectacle. The Sun, a fiery orb descending beyond the horizon, set the heavens ablaze with hues of gold and crimson, a daily masterpiece unmarred by the troubles of mere mortals.

As the light caressed the land and cast long shadows across the dunes, Hakim and Zenobia remained in silent reverence. In the solitude, their connection deepened, anchored by the simple act of watching day surrender to night. It was here, on the cusp of darkness, that they found strength in each other's presence, a bond unbroken by time or trial, woven through the very fabric of their souls.

The cooling sands cradled them as the sky deepened to a velvet canvas, punctuated by the first glimmers of starlight. Hakim would turn to Zenobia, his voice low and steady against the whispering wind, "Your courage ignites the stars themselves, my love."

She leaned into his embrace, her heart a tempest of emotions. In the quiet expanse, away from the chaos and magic that marked their days, she found solace in his unwavering presence. The warmth of his arms was an anchor in the shifting dunes of uncertainty.

"Without you, Aggrabad would be lost," he says, his words resonating with the weight of truth. "You have the soul of a Roc, mighty and free. Your strength gives this city hope."

Zenobia's eyes shimmered in the twilight, and her lips whispered a silent thank you, but no words were needed. The gratitude that filled her gaze spoke volumes, a silent testament to their shared history and the trials they had overcome together.

As night claimed the desert, Hakim would draw back slightly, and study her face as if memorizing every detail. The passion in his eyes was mirrored by the conviction in her own. In that look, there was a promise, a vow that extended beyond the boundaries of their entwined hands.

He brushed his lips against hers, a kiss as fervent as the desert sun, sealing their pact in the cool embrace of evening. It was more than a gesture of love; it was an oath of partnership, an acknowledgement of the path they would walk together.

They were close, their breath mingling with the air, their faces mere inches apart. But what they didn't know was that their world was poised on the brink of tumult, and until that day dawned, they were one. Rarely a word had to be spoken; their love was a silent vow, unspoken yet understood.

"Whatever comes, we will face it together," Hakim said, his voice firm with resolve.

"Always," Zenobia whispered back, her voice equally as steadfast.

With the Rub al-Khali as their witness, they made their way back to the city, hands joined. Their silhouettes cast long shadows across the sand, two figures ready to defend the Atlantis of the Desert, united by love and bound by duty.

An encroaching darkness threatened to engulf the land, and Hakim and Zenobia would face it with hearts ablaze, kindled by a passionate kiss and the certainty that they are not merely protectors of Aggrabad, they are its very essence.

CHAPTER 6

But now, all that has changed, and amidst the chaos caused by the sandstorm, Zenobia is busier than ever, unaware that she has come to the attention of the Vizier's guards yet again.

Hakim's heart is pounding in his chest, and each beat is like a drum of war as he keeps pace with his men. His broad shoulders brush past agitated onlookers, and his muscular build is a testament to his many years as a warrior.

He dodges a stone pot that falls from one of the crumbling walls above, and it may have done substantial damage if he had not seen it coming. His agility, honed from youth is his ally in the narrow passages that snake throughout the city.

A shout goes up from behind. The Vizier's guards have spotted Zenobia's avian form against the brilliant blue sky. They hurl threats and curses, their desperation palpable in the sweltering heat. Hakim clenches his jaw, his green eyes narrowing with determination.

"Over here, you foul beasts," he roars as he diverts the attention of the guards, thereby giving Zenobia the time she needs to gain some distance.

His hand finds the hilt of his scimitar, the cool metal a familiar comfort. With a swift motion, he draws the blade and parries a strike from an overzealous guard. The clang of steel echoes off the stone buildings, a chorus to their perilous dance.

Ever aware, Zenobia weaves through the air as a diminutive sparrow, and threads through the chaos with ease. Hakim vaults over a low wall, lands on his feet, and continues his relentless pursuit. The alleyways become a blur of shadow and light as he follows Zenobia's lead, the two of them a whirlwind of motion amidst the stillness of the desert city.

She cannot hear him crying out or what he is saying. It is more a mantra for himself, a promise that he will protect her, no matter what. Together, they twist and turn throughout the city, its pulse racing alongside their own.

The marketplace is no longer a riot of color and sound, just a labyrinth of broken stalls and canvas awnings under which merchants used to hawk their wares. The cacophony of vendors and the fragrant tang of spices no longer hangs thick in the air,

A sudden gust of wind stops the guards for a fleeting moment, and Zenobia expands in mid-flight, the diminutive sparrow disappears and she changes into the powerful shape of a falcon.

Her transformation is a blur of feathers and light, a testament to the mystical power she wields. With a piercing cry, she soars upward, her keen eyes scanning for threats from high above the tumult.

People are doing their best to salvage whatever they can. "Make way," Hakim cries, his voice resonating with the authority of his station. The crowd shuffles and jostles, some glancing up to catch sight of the majestic bird now circling overhead. Hakim pushes on, the golden Sun reflecting off the hilt of his scimitar that rests at his side.

Amidst the din, one of the Vizier's guards spots the falcon's shadow flitting across the sky, and, with a calculating eye, he readies his bow. Zenobia's sharp instincts sense the danger; her wings beat rapidly as she seeks to gain altitude but it's too late. The guard manages to clip one of her wings, and a handful of tail feathers fall to the ground.

"Zenobia," Hakim cries, panic edging his voice. She plummets to the earth, squealing like an injured bird, a sound that cuts through the marketplace and pierces Hakim's heart.

He springs into action and leaps onto a vendor's cart in front of the guards and blinds them momentarily with a cascade of over-ripe dates.

Then, he vaults onto a loose wooden beam so that he can catch Zenobia before anything happens. And as she descends in a wild spiral, Hakim extends his arms hoping to catch her. Time slows, and his eyes lock onto hers. The falcon falls into his open arms, and with a masterful roll, he absorbs the impact, and cradles the precious bird against his chest. They slide across the awning and come to rest at its edge.

For a moment, all is still. Hakim gets to his feet and sets Zenobia down. Her feathers, once ruffled with distress, now lay smooth as she regains her composure. A shared look of silent communication follows, one that speaks of trust forged in fire and adversity.

"Are you hurt?" he says softly, his commanding tone replaced with concern.

With a gentle shake of her head, Zenobia reassures him that she isn't, her brown eyes glistening with gratitude. Her gaze holds his own, conveying a depth of emotion in a singular connection.

With Zenobia secure at his side, he surveys the path ahead, knowing that each step they take defies the destiny that others seek to impose. Together, they are unbreakable: a captain of the guards and a daughter of magic, two against the world.

With the clamor of pursuit fading into the labyrinth of the streets, Hakim takes her to a secluded alcove behind a cascading bougainvillea vine. The vibrant flowers hang like a veil, ensuring their momentary seclusion from the eyes of the world. Their chests heave in unison, breaths coming in short gasps as the adrenaline of the chase slowly ebbs away.

"That was a close one," Hakim sighs, his voice tinged with relief as he leans back against the cool limestone wall. He watches Zenobia closely; her transformation from falcon to woman is always seamless, silent, and beautiful.

"Yes, but we have to be more careful," she says as she tucks a loose strand of hair behind her ear. Her laughter is light, almost musical, yet it carries the weight of their shared ordeals.

Hakim's eyes soften as he gazes at her face, a quality that defines him in battle but one that also gives way to tenderness.

"Do you remember the time we snuck into the gardens of the Grand Vizier?" he said, his voice dipping into reminiscence. "We were no older than the street urchins and just as mischievous."

Zenobia's eyes sparkle with fondness and light up with the memory. "How could I forget? You dared me to steal a pomegranate from his prized tree." Her laughter echoes again, and bounces softly off the alcove walls. "And when we were caught, you took the blame. You said it was your idea all along."

"Because it was," Hakim says, as he shares an affectionate smile. "Even then, you had a way of making every reckless plan seem worth it."

She moves in closer, her presence a comforting warmth amidst the desert chill that is creeping in with the dusk. "And you always had a way of protecting me, even before I had the power of the Roc."

Their eyes meet, and in that gaze are unspoken words, a history rich with adventure, loyalty, and an affection that has blossomed over many years of camaraderie. It's a bond that neither time nor turmoil could ever tarnish, and in that hidden alcove, the chaos of Aggrabad seems worlds away.

"Whatever happens now," Hakim says, his hand finding hers, "we will face it together, as we always have."

"And we always will," she says, her fingers tightening around his. Her eyes mirror the resolve that shines in his soul, and in that quiet moment, shielded by the city they have vowed to protect, they find solace in each other's company, a captain and an enchantress bound by history and the unyielding promise of their intertwined destinies.

A respite in the alcove lasts but a few heartbeats before Zenobia's playful spirit takes flight. With a glimmer in her deep brown eyes and a mischievous smile curving her lips, she transforms into a tiny hummingbird. Her wings beat with rapid grace, and the iridescence of her feathers catch the fading sunlight as she flutters around Hakim's head.

He reaches out with a gentle hand, his fingers brushing the delicate softness of her plumage. "You always find a way to lighten the moment," he says, his voice laced with fondness. The air thrums with the hum of her wings, a melody that speaks of freedom and joy, even amidst the danger that exists all around.

"Is it not easier to face darkness with lightness in one's heart," she chirps, her voice musical even in such a little body. She darts close enough for Hakim to feel the whisper of air displaced by her tiny wings.

"Ah, but who will keep us grounded if you are always taking to the skies?" Hakim says teasingly, his eyes following her as she dances through the air.

"Oh, Hakim, we were never meant for the ground," Zenobia replies, her laughter tinkling like silver bells. "We were meant to soar like eagles."

CHAPTER 7

The following day is another day of heartbreak and turmoil. And as he works away with his men in the scorching heat of a courtyard, Hakim looks up, only to discover that he is surrounded by a contingent of the Vizier's guards.

The limestone walls of the palace reflects the light in a blinding cascade, but it is not the heat that causes beads of sweat to form on his men's brows. It is the presence of the Vizier who approaches with an air of disdain that seems to wilt the tapestries that still line the walls.

"Captain Al-Rashid," he says with a distinctive sneer, his voice cutting through the silence like a scimitar's edge. "Your defiance has not gone unnoticed. Tell me, do you serve the Sultan, or do you serve your misguided conscience?"

Hakim's eyes remain steady as he faces the Vizier, his posture as unyielding as the desert palms.

"I serve Sultan Mahmoud ibn Khaleed, as is my sworn duty. My actions are for the safety and prosperity of Aggrabad and her people."

"Your duty," the Vizier says mockingly as he circles Hakim like a jackal. "That's a convenient excuse for insubordination. Your loyalty should be absolute, Captain. The Sultan's will is Aggrabad's lifeblood."

"True loyalty does not blind one to the plight of the innocent," Hakim replies, his tone even. "It demands that we uphold justice, even when doing so challenges us the most."

The Vizier pauses before such insolence, his opulent robes glistening with malice. "You dare speak of justice? In these times, it is power that reigns supreme. Remember that, Captain, lest you find yourself on the wrong side of the Sultan's favor."

"Justice is power," Hakim counters firmly, his resolve reflecting the unwavering spirit of Aggrabad itself. "And I stand by it, as I stand by the people who look to us for protection. That is the foundation upon which this city was built."

With a scoff, the Vizier looks away momentarily, his arrogance leaving a sour trail in the hot air. Hakim watches closely, knowing that the battle for Aggrabad's soul is just beginning.

The stillness of the moment shatters like fragile glass as the Vizier's venomous words slither through the air once again. "Your virtue blinds you, Hakim," he says sneeringly, a wicked smile curling his lips. "But let us see how well it serves you when those you hold dear suffer for your obstinacy."

Hakim's heart thunders against his chest, and a foreboding chill creeps across his skin. "What have you done?" he demands to know, his voice betraying more than a hint of trepidation.

The Vizier's eyes gleam with malevolent satisfaction. "A simple demonstration of consequences," he replies, drawing out each syllable as if he is unsheathing a scimitar. "While you parade your precious honor before the Sultan's court, I took the liberty of securing your family within the cold embrace of the dungeon. Consider it an incentive to realign your priorities."

Shock flashes across Hakim's face. The color drains from his cheeks as the magnitude of the Vizier's betrayal sinks its cruel talons deep into his soul. He clenches his hands into a fist, his knuckles whiten with restrained fury. The dungeon, the darkness, the clink of chains, and the terrified whispers of his loved ones coalesce in his mind igniting a fire that threatens to eat away at his composure.

Perched upon a windowsill, Zenobia is disguised as a small bird and observes this situation with an intensity that belies its delicate form. Her heart races beneath her feathered breast, her keen eyes fixed on Hakim's stricken face.

The Vizier's guards had dragged his unsuspecting family out of their home and herded them off to the dungeon, their pleas muffled by the walls in which they are now imprisoned.

Zenobia's beak opens slightly as if to call out, but she remains silent, a guardian whose presence goes unnoticed by all but the desert wind. The weight of responsibility presses down upon her soul. As she knows, only a bird can navigate the labyrinth of corridors and help Hakim find his family.

As the Vizier strides away with a triumphant swish of robes, he leaves a palpable tension hanging in the air. Zenobia flutters down from her perch and circles above Hakim's head. Desperate and broken, he stands like a solitary pillar amidst the chaos of betrayal.

Zenobia's sharp eyes never waver and her resolve is as firm as the ancient stones of Aggrabad. She will be the whisper of hope in the dark, the ally that Hakim needs in his most desperate hour.

She descends with the grace of a majestic and imposing desert falcon and sweeps down to Hakim, who remains rooted to the ground. His men watch their Captain with uncertainty.

"Captain," Zenobia says as her voice pierces the turmoil within, her words crisp and urgent as they always are in moments of crisis. "It is true; your family is confined in the depths of the Sultan's dungeon."

Hakim's fists are still clenched at his side. The shock of the Vizier's revelation is still fresh on his mind, compounded by Zenobia's confirmation. He struggles to maintain his composure under the gaze of his loyal soldiers, aware that any sign of weakness could sow seeds of doubt about his leadership.

"Are you certain," he says, though the question is needless. Even in her avian form, Zenobia's eyes bear the weight of truth. "By my life, I am," she says with a solemn nod. "You must act swiftly, Hakim."

The urgency in her tone is a clarion call, but it clashes with the oath he took as the Captain of the Guards, the oath to serve Aggrabad above all else. Yet, how can he stand idly by while his own blood suffer at the hands of a tyrant?

"Zenobia," he cries, struggling to keep his voice steady. I cannot abandon my post, not when the city teeters on the edge of chaos."

His heart is racing and a storm of conflicting loyalties threaten to tear him apart. Duty, honor, and love pull at him with the might of a Karkadann, the fiercest of all unicorns. The thought of his family locked away in some fetid cell makes his stomach churn. But if he forsakes his responsibilities, what then? Will Aggrabad fall into ruin?

"Yet, how can I claim to protect this city when I cannot even protect my kin?" he cries, more to himself than to Zenobia, his gaze losing focus as he stares into the void. His mind conjures up images of his father, who had once stood where he stands now, a paragon of virtue.

"What would he have done?"

"Think, Hakim," he urges himself silently. "There must be a way to uphold your duty to both."

An inner battle rages as fiercely as any he has ever had to deal with before. With each passing moment, the knowledge that his family languishes in darkness gnaws at him, yet the consequences of his absence from the city's defenses are equally dire.

"Time runs thin like the dunes in a tempest," Zenobia says as she studies him closely, her gaze piercing the armor of the vulnerable man beneath.

"Indeed," Hakim says, his resolve hardening like the stone walls of Aggrabad itself. "We must follow a path that walks the edge of a blade and of these perils."

Resolved, his piercing eyes come alive with fierce determination and the pain of his predicament. He will stand true to his name and lineage and find a way to save his family without forsaking his sacred duty to the city he swore to defend.

His hand hovers over the hilt of his sword, a silent sentinel at his side. The weight of command feels heavier than ever as he grapples with the Vizier's betrayal and his family's imprisonment. Zenobia's presence is a balm to his troubled spirit; their bond, an unspoken vow of unity against the shadows that threaten Aggrabad.

"Hakim, even the mightiest dunes shift with the wind," Zenobia says, her voice a gentle melody that soothes his fraying resolve. "Let not your heart be a fortress against your own blood. I stand with you, as certain as the moon guides the night."

Hakim meets her gaze and finds solace in the depths of her deep brown eyes. Her confidence, a beacon in the encroaching darkness, fuels his courage.

"Zenobia, your faith is the star that guides me through this abyss. My family's safety is the wind upon which our future rests. Their freedom will be a clarion call that rallies our people against this tyranny."

"Then let us not delay," she says, as her hand brushes against his arm, a touch as light as a feather yet grounded in strength. "This night, we carve a path not just through stone and mortar but through fear and despair."

"Indeed," Hakim says, his voice resolute as he draws himself up to his full height. "We shall strike swiftly, like the falcon in its hunt. The Sultan's trust in me shall not be misplaced, nor shall my kin suffer while I draw breath."

"Your father's honor lives within you, Hakim Al-Rashid," Zenobia says. "Together, we shall restore balance to the scales of justice."

"Then it will be, by the ancient pact of Aggrabad and the sacred oath of my lineage," Hakim vows, his words cutting through the stillness of the night, "I shall return my family to the light. And woe unto those who stand in my way."

Under the cover of a moonless night, they huddle in the shadow of a date palm, their voices barely audible over the murmuring wind. The limestone walls of the palace loom ahead, bathed in an ethereal glow from torches that flicker like fireflies caught in a giant's snare.

"A pair of guards patrol the eastern wing at fifteen-minute intervals," Hakim says as his mind maps out the dungeons of the palace. "We must exploit the opportunity to act when the guard changes; that's when their vigilance wanes."

Zenobia nods, her eyes reflecting the determination that matches his own. "And the song of the Shadhavar will ensnare them in its spell, buying us precious time," she says with tactical acuity.

"Indeed," he says, "but we dare not risk your transformation under such scrutiny. Your avian guise will be our eyes from above. Signal me should danger approach."

"Be wary of the Nasnas lurking in the shadows; they possess senses keener than any mortal's," she says, her voice a silken thread binding them to caution.

"Then it is settled," Hakim says as he adjusts the scimitar at his side, its blade an extension of his resolve. "We navigate the arteries of the palace as silent as the desert breeze until we reach the heart of the dungeon."

They slip through an archway, the fragrance of exotic spices lingering in the air as if to bid them farewell on their perilous journey. Zenobia perches upon a balustrade, spreads her wings, now those of a small sparrow, and flies upward, a guardian spirit cloaked in feathers.

Hakim moves with the stealth of a panther, his form melds with the shifting patterns of light and dark. Every step is measured, and every breath is controlled. His keen gaze flickers from alcove to corridor, alert to any sign of movement.

The sound of shuffling feet alerts him to the sound of the approaching guards. He presses himself against an ornate tapestry, their threads tell tales of ancient heroes whose valor seeps into his very soul.

The guards pass by, their laughter discordant in the night's symphony. A subtle chirp from Zenobia signals the all-clear, and Hakim makes his move, his presence no more than a whisper against the cool stone floor.

As they navigate the labyrinth beneath the palace, Zenobia guides him past pockets of danger. A guard rounds the corner unexpectedly and Hakim takes cover as if he is a part of the very dungeon itself. With a swift dive, Zenobia distracts the guard by rustling a lantern, long enough for Hakim to vanish into the shadows once more.

Finally, they arrive at the mouth of despair, the entrance to the dungeon. Its heavy door stands before them, a mute sentinel that guards sorrow in its iron-clad jaws. Here, the stakes are high and the dance with danger most intimate. Hakim can hear the muffled cries of the imprisoned, each one a dagger twisting in his heart.

"Be swift, Hakim; the night ages and dawn will soon cast its judging eye," Zenobia whispers, her form human once again as she joins him in the flesh.

"By the morrow, these walls shall echo with songs of freedom, not lament," he says as he reaches for the door with hands that tremble not from fear but from a fervent desire to mend what has been unjustly broken.

The lock yields, his skillful touch has set many unfortunate people free before this night. With a final glance shared between two souls fused by purpose, Hakim steps into the belly of the beast, an unyielding force for justice in the heart of Aggrabad.

His shadow merges with the darkness as he stalks the corridor, each movement a silent promise of his resolve. The flicker of torches cast an erratic glow, but to the Captain of the Guards, the shadows are allies, whispering secrets of unseen paths.

A guard looms ahead but his back is turned, a mistake that will cost him dearly. Hakim inches closer, his breath a controlled hush against the still air. He wraps a powerful arm around the guard's neck and applies pressure at just the right spot. The man's body goes limp, unconscious but unharmed. Hakim lowers him to the ground with a gentleness that one might not expect of a seasoned warrior.

He moves on without pause, each step brings him closer to the heavy iron bars that imprison his family. Another sentry blocks his way, the clink of armor betraying his position.

Hakim draws a small pouch from his belt and tosses it in one fluid motion. The concoction bursts into a cloud of pungent smoke and engulfs the guard, who coughs and staggers, his senses overwhelmed. Hakim seizes the moment, disarms the man with a deft twist, and sends him to dream among the sands.

The dungeon door now stands before him, its ominous presence a mere footnote in this odyssey. He presses his ear against the cold metal, listening for the rhythm of life.

A faint sob reaches his ears, and one that pierces his warrior's façade. It is the voice of his mother. His fingers trace the ancient words etched into the door, each one a symbol, a testament to his city's storied past, and now, the barrier between him and his kin.

Hakim takes a deep breath to steels his nerves and pushes the door, and the creaking of the hinges resound with a prelude to salvation. His eyes take a moment to adjust to the gloom, and then he sees his family. Shackled and weary, they lift their heads in disbelief. The sight of his loved ones in chains ignites a flame within, yet Hakim's approach is measured, his presence a soothing balm.

"Mother," he cries. All titles fall away in an instant. He is no longer a captain; he is simply her son, Hakim, a man whose world has been torn asunder and is now slowly coming back together.

He kneels before his mother, his broad hands working quickly to unlock the shackles with keys procured from fallen jailers. As each lock clicks open, a weight lifts from his soul.

His little sister throws her tiny arms around his neck, and the tears that have been held at bay break free, and carve warm trails down his weathered cheeks.

"Shh, my little dove," he says soothingly, his voice barely above a whisper. His touch is tender as he brushes away her tears, and then turns to embrace his mother.

Her strength has always been the quiet anchor in his turbulent world. His younger brother, Mahdi, proud and brave, joins in the embrace. Their unity is impenetrable even when faced with the darkest forms of magic.

"Freedom is ours once again," he cries, the timbre of his voice promising retribution and the warmth of home. "Together, we shall rise above the shadows."

In that dungeon, amidst the echoes of despair, Hakim Al-Rashid holds his family close, their bonds unbroken, their spirits unbound. There is no time for lingering, no room for doubt, only the certainty of their courage and a love that binds them tighter than any chain ever could.

Hakim takes them by the hand and guides them through the labyrinth that is the dungeon. The air hangs heavy with dampness, and the pale light from hidden alcoves cast eerie shadows along the walls. Zenobia, her keen eyes attuned to the subtleties of the darkness flies ahead like a wraith, her avian senses alert to any other sound.

"Stay close," Hakim whispers, his hushed words barely rustling the silence. His family, accustomed to tales of his valor but unversed in the art of stealth, mimic his every move, their steps cautious upon the ancient stones. With each turn they take, the oppressive weight of the fortress seems to bear down upon them as if the very walls have a desire to keep their secrets.

The air grows cooler as they ascend, and at the final corridor, they feel a faint draft of cool air. Zenobia pauses, and tilts her head to listen. "This way," she whispers, her voice carrying the certainty of the wind itself. Hakim nods, he trusts her instincts implicitly, and leads his family down the chosen path.

They enter a vaulted chamber where the distant glimmer of moonlight beckons like a beacon of hope. Zenobia returns to her human guise and tests the barred window above but finds that it will not yield.

"Here," Hakim says as he boosts his brother up to reach the bars. And with Zenobia's guidance, Mahdi undoes the latch that holds the shutters closed. A rush of cool night air that carries the scent of jasmine and freedom floods the chamber.

As they squeeze through the opening one at a time, Hakim turns to Zenobia with eyes that speak of his gratitude. "Without you, this night would have seen the end of my legacy," he says, his voice a low thrum in the stillness. "You have my eternal thanks, Zenobia al-Farsi."

She meets his gaze, her eyes reflecting the moon's soft luminescence. "There is no debt between us, Hakim," she replies, her tone imbued with warmth. "For family and for Aggrabad, we stand united." Her hand reaches out, and her fingers brush against his in a gesture of solidarity.

"United," he says as he clasps her hand firmly before they slip through the window and leave the dark confines of the dungeon behind.

As they navigate the palace grounds, the guards who patrol the periphery are oblivious to the events unfolding beneath the cloak of night. Hakim's heart races, not from fear but from the exhilarating proximity to salvation. They are but shadows drifting through the tapestry of Aggrabad's soul, bound to one another by purpose and perseverance.

They finally arrive at a door on the outskirts of the walls, one that is hidden amongst palm fronds and the ever rising sand. Hakim allows himself a moment to take a breath. He looks to Zenobia, her presence a constant comfort. He knows that they have turned the tide of destiny in their favor.

Hakim leads his family through the labyrinth of alleys and side streets that snake throughout a city which sleeps under a blanket of stars, unaware of what is unfolding in its heart.

They head off into the night and leave the palace walls far behind. Zenobia's keen eyes are constantly searching for any sign of pursuit. She is ever vigilant and keeps pace with Hakim and his family as they hasten away from danger.

"Stay low," Hakim whispers quietly. His siblings, their eyes wide with the residue of fear nod silently. His mother's hand clutches at his arm. Her strength falters, but her spirit is unbroken. They trust Hakim implicitly, and at this time, their faith is a weighty mantle upon his shoulders.

"Turn here," Zenobia says, as she leads them down an even narrower passage to where the scent of jasmine lingers in the air, a silent testament to the life that thrives in Aggrabad's hidden corners.

They emerge on the outskirts of the city, where the sands stretch out like an endless sea. Here, the cool night breeze carries the whisper of freedom and the promise of dawn's light.

"Once we cross the dunes, we will be beyond the Vizier's reach," Hakim assures his loved ones, though the statement is as much for himself as it is for them.

They pause and look back at the place they once called home. In the silver glow of the moon, what is left of Aggrabad stands serene and timeless, its beauty almost lost and subdued by the desert sand and the malice that festers within.

"Aggrabad will be safe again," Hakim vows, more to the wind than anyone else. "We shall return and cleanse it of this foul and horrible creature."

"You will," his sister whispers, her voice steady despite the shadows beneath her eyes.

"Let us move," Zenobia says, her gaze fixed on the horizon. "Our path lies ahead, and time is not our ally."

They head off into the desert, their steps quiet on the soft sand. Hakim feels the weight of his sword at his side, and beside him is Zenobia; her presence, a beacon of hope, her resilience mirroring his own.

As they traverse the dunes, the first hint of purple and orange streak through the sky, heralding the approach of morning. Their journey is far from over, but Hakim knows that each step will take his family away from the Vizier and closer to salvation.

With the palace now nothing more than a distant dream, they vanish into the burgeoning dawn, their silhouettes melting into the vast expanse of the desert. Ahead lies uncertainty and the unyielding resolve to fight for what is right, for freedom, and for the future.

CHAPTER 8

Now that his mother and siblings are safe and far away from all of that tumult, Hakim takes his leave and promises that he will return.

He and Zenobia have no choice but to return to Aggrabad, and with the stealth of a mouse, they venture into the secret passageways beneath the Vizier's private domain.

With the grace of a desert panther, Hakim leads his men through the labyrinthine corridors, their steps muted by the tapestries that line the ancient walls.

"Be careful," he whispers, his voice barely audible, "the Djinn are not the only ones who have ears."

His men nod quietly, their hands resting on the hilts of their swords, their eyes alert. They are an elite force who were chosen for their valor and discretion, each one as familiar with the hidden arteries of the palace as the streets of Aggrabad itself.

They arrive at the Vizier's quarters, where the air is heavy with exotic spices. His chamber is in darkness, except for a single flickering oil lamp that casts a dancing shadow across the furniture.

"Search everywhere," Hakim says, as his eyes scan the chamber for any sign of danger. "Leave no scroll unturned, no artifact unchecked. We seek the truth behind Memphalut's duplicity."

With movements honed by years of military precision, his men disperse and investigate every nook and cranny for any hint of concealed compartments or hidden levers. They search behind every tapestry and the intricate carvings on each piece of furniture. Their caution is palpable; they know of the Dark Conjurer's reputation for traps and enchantments all too well.

Hakim approaches a massive desk, its surface littered with scrolls and parchments. He sifts through each of the parchments, his brow knitted as he searches for anything out of place. Every so often, he glances at the Vizier's staff which rests against a desk. It's a sinister thing topped with a crystal skull that seems to be watching his every move with its cold glass gaze.

"Captain," one of his men says from the far corner of the room. "There's something peculiar about this wall hanging."

Hakim studies an embroidered depiction of a Shadhavar, its horn embedded with silver thread seems to shimmer in the lamplight and sing a silent song of enchantment.

"Let's see what's behind it," he says as he pushes it to the side, only to discover a slight indentation in the wall. And with a gentle push, the wall gives way, only to reveal a hollow space beyond.

"Memphalut's secrets begin to unravel," Hakim says, his heart pounding with the promise of dark revelations and the gravity of what they might uncover. He signals his men to continue the search, knowing that time is as much a foe as the Vizier himself.

Hakim is all too conscious of the weight of responsibility bearing down on him. Every second that ticks by feels like an eternity, and every creak is a potential alarm. Yet, they persevere, united by their dedication to unearth the treachery that threatens to engulf their beloved city.

Hakim's gaze sweeps over the expanse of the Vizier's quarters, his eyes focused on anything unusual. The air is thick with the aroma of exotic incense, a feeble attempt to mask the stench of dark sorcery that seems almost palpable. Every step they take is a silent testament to their vigilance, every breath a guarded secret that might produce a result.

Hakim's keen eyes settle on an ornate bookshelf laden with leather-bound tomes and scrolls sealed with wax emblems, all of which whisper ominously of hidden knowledge. This collection goes way beyond mere decoration or scholarly pursuit; it's a repository for power that could bind the Djinn and command the Falak in its fiery wrath.

Hakim follows the path of an intricate pattern until he finds a cleverly disguised lever between the spines of two ancient texts. With a deep breath that does little to steady his racing pulse, he exerts a subtle pressure on the lever. A soft click echoes through the chamber and a section of the shelf recedes with a hush, only to reveal a compartment lined with papyrus so old that they might crumble at a touch.

This is obviously forbidden knowledge, scrolls etched with runes that dance and writhe like living shadows, texts that speak of unspeakable rituals, their very presence a defilement of all things pure.

"That is dark magic," says one of his men.

"Indeed," Hakim says, his voice barely a whisper. "The Vizier's heresy goes deeper than we feared."

As they absorb the gravity of their find, a low rumble resonates from the opposite end of the room. Hakim turns to see one of his most trusted soldiers pressing against a seemingly innocuous segment of the wall. Stone grinds against stone, and a hidden door opens, beckoning them into the mouth of secrets yet untold.

"By the Karkadann's horn," another soldier swears as he peers into the darkness beyond.

"Steady," Hakim says as he steels himself for what lies ahead. Their torches cast a flickering light that barely illuminates a repository of horrors.

What greets them is a tableau of nightmares made manifest. Artifacts of bone and blood, amulets that thrum with malevolent energy, and symbols scrawled in crimson upon the walls. Each of which is a testament to the Vizier's allegiance to forces that should never be named. And at the center of it all stands an altar, its surface stained with the echoes of countless vile supplications.

"Memphalut al Shikari is a demon," Hakim cries, as he brandishes his name like a curse, his hands clenching into fists. "He seeks to unmake the world that we hold dear, to bend the will of the Djinn and demons alike to his twisted desires."

The men share a look of grim determination. Their loyalty to their Captain and to Aggrabad burns as fiercely as the desert sun. They are not just soldiers; they are guardians standing on the precipice of a war waged in shadow and deceit. And Hakim, their unwavering leader, will guide them through the tempest that looms on the horizon.

Hakim investigates the lines of an intricate carving on one of the carved wooden chests, and is conscious of the dark energy that emanates from within. The chest is crafted from ebony and reinforced with bands of iron, its surface etched with symbols that whisper of ancient, forbidden knowledge. The lock is a complex mechanism that would stymie any common thief, but it's no match for Hakim's battle-honed instincts.

"Stand back," he says to his men in hushed tones. With a swift kick, the sound of splintered wood echoes through the silence as the lock gives way and reveals the secrets it has guarded so jealously.

Wrapped in velvet is a map wrought with meticulous precision. The streets and alleys of Aggrabad are inked onto the parchment, and converge on the Sultan's palace. But this is not just a map. This is a plan, a blueprint for treachery. Lines snake across the paper marking secret passages and hidden doors, each path leading to the heart of the Sultan's domain.

"By the light of the Shadhavar," Hakim cries as he studies the web of deceit. The Vizier seeks to enthrone himself amidst blood and betrayal."

His men crowd around, their faces grim as they grasp the gravity of what they behold, but there is more. Beneath the map is a stack of papers that attracts Hakim's attention. The chill he feels has little to do with the cold stone beneath his feet.

"Captain," one of his soldiers says, "what further evil has this man wrought?"

Hakim unfolds one of the pages with a reverence that belies his anger, his eyes scanning the spidery script. Detailed with a scholar's obsession are accounts of experiments most foul, of beggar after beggar who was lured into the Vizier's domain with promises of gold, only to become the subject of dark rites. Names and dates are recorded with a detachment that chills the blood, each entry a life stolen, a spirit broken under the Vizier's cruel hand.

"May the Djinn take him," Hakim swears, his voice heavy with sorrow for the lost and rage for the perpetrator. "He has made pawns of the poorest, those already weighed down by the Sultan's tyranny."

A fire kindles within Hakim's breast, one that rekindles a legacy of power that he has never used before. "It is time to bring an end to the Vizier's machinations," he says. It is more than duty that drives Hakim now. Justice is the power that sustains the Captain of the Guards.

"Let these be the last victims of his ambition," Hakim declares. "We shall strike at that serpent before it can poison the throne, and we will shield Aggrabad from the encroaching darkness."

With the weight of destiny upon their shoulders, Hakim and his men prepare to face the treacherous road ahead. They will need all of their courage and cunning, for the Vizier is a master of shadows, and they have just stepped into his lair.

The moon hangs low, a pale sentinel in the night sky, as Zenobia's sharp gaze sweeps over the walls of Aggrabad. The soft rustle of date palms whispers it secrets to those who will listen. From her vantage point, she can see the guards patrolling down below, their spears glinting under the evening sky.

"Roc's eyes," she says. This is a power that invokes her mystical kinship with the legendary eagle and sharpens her vision. She knows that time is slipping through their fingers like sand in an hourglass.

"Be swift," she whispers as she holds a small stone in her hand, its surface etched with symbols that pulse with a faint blue glow. This is a charm, a gift from an aging sorcerer, and it is the perfect way to send an urgent message directly to Hakim's mind.

Hakim places one hand above a stack of parchments and stops. The stone at his neck is warm against his skin and vibrates with Zenobia's warning. His heart quickens, but his voice is a calm whisper as he addresses his men. "The guards are restless. We must hasten our search."

The urgency lends them haste without chaos, their movements precise and deliberate. Behind a tapestry woven with the exploits of ancient heroes, Hakim discovers another hidden door. A faint draught teases the edges of the fabric, and the air tastes of secrets long buried.

"Here," he says as he presses against the stonework. The wall yields, only to reveal a narrow passage that descends into darkness. He exchanges a look of uncertainty with his men, the silent communication of warriors prepared for the unknown.

Torches in hand, they follow the hidden stairwell, their boots silent against the cold stone floor. The air grows cooler, damper, as if the earth itself is breathing.

At the base of the steps, they find an underground chamber shrouded in shadows. The flickering torchlight dances across the space and reveals something terrifying, the remnants of a dark ritual. In the center of the room stands a sacrificial altar, stark against the surrounding darkness, its stone surface stained with the remains of innocent blood.

A closer investigation reveals symbols carved into the altar, arcane and twisted, pulsing with a malevolence that seems to claw at the edge of their mind. Around it lay scattered remnants, candles burnt down to the stubs, bowls caked with dried herbs, and bones that glisten in the torchlight.

"This is Memphalut al Shikari's work," Hakim cries, the name leaving a bitter taste on his tongue. The very air of the chamber is charged with the Dark Conjurer's presence, heavy with the residue of incantations most foul.

"Let no part of this escape your scrutiny," Hakim says, his voice a low growl. "Every clue we unearth brings us closer to thwarting his vile ambitions."

His men spread out and examine every crevice with the meticulous care of a jeweler appraising a diamond. Hakim approaches the altar, his hands steady despite the revulsion inside. He will not flinch from the darkness; he will drag it into the light and burn it away with the fire of justice.

Aggrabad's fate hangs in the balance, and Hakim Al-Rashid will not and cannot falter. An invisible power infects the air like a cold embrace. Each artifact within the chamber seems to pulse with its own sinister life force, and casts elongated shadows on the walls that dance mockingly in the torchlight.

"There's something else here," one of his men says. His hand strays towards the hilt of his scimitar as if steel could ward off an unseen menace.

"Not so loud," Hakim cautions him through gritted teeth, his instincts telling him they are far from alone in this profane sanctuary. Eyes narrowed, he peruses the arcane symbols, each a testament to the Vizier's betrayal. It is as if the very essence of the Djinn had been perverted in this chamber, their elemental magic twisted into something grotesque.

It is then that they hear the distant echo of footsteps, a rhythmic cadence that grows steadily louder. With a swift motion of his hand, Hakim signals his men to find a hiding place. They move with the silence of desert phantoms, and find refuge behind columns and alcoves.

Hakim watches as the ornate door creaks open, and then the Vizier appears, clad in a robe that shimmers with threads of obsidian. He approaches the altar with reverent steps, and in his hand, he clutches an ancient scepter, mounted by a gemstone with an ominous glow.

The Vizier begins to chant in a language older than the dunes themselves, each syllable laced with a power that pulls at the fabric of the world. The malevolent energy that permeates the room coalesces around him, responding to his command. Patterns of light skitter across the floor, converging on the altar where shadows writhe as if they were alive.

Hakim's heart is pounding in his ears, not just from the fear of discovery but from the realization of what this means. Should this ritual reach its completion, it will seal the fate of the Sultan and all of Aggrabad. He can almost feel the powerful energy of the Karkadann in the shadows, but he is prepared to strike against such evil.

As the Vizier raises the scepter high, the chamber responds with a surge of wind which snuffs out the torches and leaves only the cold luminescence of sorcery. Hidden in the darkness, Hakim feels his resolve as a warrior harden within. No matter the might of the Falak or the cunning of the Nasnas, he will stand against this darkness.

For now, he and his men remain unseen, mere ghosts in the shadow of the Vizier's ambition. Hakim makes a silent vow: The truth will blaze forth like the desert sun and banish the corruption that seeks to choke the life from the city that he swore to protect.

Beneath the trembling light of dark enchantments, he watches with a smoldering rage as the Vizier's gestures weave spells of treachery and malevolence. Each incantation that slips from his lips, every blasphemous symbol he traces in the air is a lash against the fabric of Aggrabad's fate. This ancient chamber, hidden deep beneath the palace, bears witness to an unforgivable betrayal.

Hakim's fists are clenched so tightly that his nails are biting into his palms, the pain a mere echo of the fury that scorches in his veins. He has seen enough; the evidence is damning, but this vile ritual is an affront to everything sacred.

As the shadow of the Vizier dances grotesquely on the walls, Hakim's resolve crystallises. He will cut through this web of deceit, even if it means walking through fire. Aggrabad will not fall while blood courses through his veins.

Then, as suddenly as it had started, this twisted rite reaches an end. The chant dwindles into silence, leaving only the heavy, expectant air of the chamber. With the arrogance of one who believes himself unseen, the Vizier wraps his cloak about his shoulders and departs, and leaves the door ajar.

Hakim signals to his men, and like phantoms, they emerge from their hiding places. Their movements are deliberate and cautious, and each step is a silent pact to carry the weight of truth back to the surface.

As they ascend the narrow winding passage that burrows ever upwards like the lair of some forgotten desert serpent, the stolen darkness of the underground gives way to the familiar night sky.

The Captain leads his men through the corridors with the surety of one who knows these stones. He could navigate blindfolded if he had to, but tonight, he moves with eyes wide and senses alert. Each man carries a piece of evidence, a shard of the puzzle that will reveal a picture of corruption so profound that it threatens to engulf the city they love.

"Quickly, but with care," Hakim says, his voice barely audible above the rustling of their robes. "We must reach the Sultan before sunrise."

The urgency of their mission lends speed to their steps, yet Hakim knows that caution is as necessary as haste. They are harbingers of a dawn that could either herald salvation or destruction for Aggrabad, depending on the swiftness of their feet and the strength of their resolve.

When they finally emerge into the cool night, the stars blink unassumingly, unaware of the mortal struggles below. Their silent vigil is a testament to their duty, and as guardians of the night, they will see them through until the light of a new day brings a new revelation and, with it hope.

Zenobia's silhouette merges with the shadows of the date palms, her eyes are fixed on the white limestone walls where hidden treacheries have been unearthed. The desert night envelops her shoulders like a calm whisper brushing against her cheek as she waits for Hakim and his men to reappear. A moment later, they appear out of the darkness, their presence a silent testament to a successful subterfuge.

"Captain," Zenobia says quietly as she steps forward to greet Hakim and his men. Her sharp and discerning gaze takes in the grave expressions etched on the faces of his warriors.

He acknowledges her presence with a nod, but his countenance bears the weight of dire revelations, and his jaw is set in grim determination.

"The Vizier's treachery runs deeper than we feared."

"Speak not here," Zenobia says, her voice a hushed melody in the stillness. "Eyes and ears may linger where they are least welcome."

Heeding her caution, they withdraw to a secluded alcove, away from prying eyes. There, beneath a celestial tapestry, Hakim reveals the map that he liberated from the Vizier's chest, a parchment inscribed with sinister intent.

"See this here," he says, as he points to the intricate markings, his finger tracing the outline of a route leading to the dark heart of the mountains. "The Vizier seeks an alliance with forces that would see Aggrabad fall into shadow."

Zenobia's deep brown eyes study the map, her lips pressed into a thin line. "Then we must seek out the old sorcerer. His wisdom is our only beacon against such darkness."

"Indeed, we should," Hakim says as he folds the map and tucks it securely inside his robe. "But the journey will be perilous and shrouded by enchantments."

"Then let us prepare," Zenobia says, her voice unwavering in its conviction, her spirit undaunted by the road ahead. "I will gather supplies, water for our thirst, dates for sustenance, and talismans to ward off evil spirits."

Hakim's respect for her fortitude grows with every passing day; Zenobia is as steadfast as the ancient walls of the city.

"And I shall assemble weapons, scimitars honed to a razor's edge and bows strung as tight as the strings of fate," he says. "We shall be armed against both mortal and Djinn alike."

"Time flees from us, Captain," she says, her eyes reflecting the urgency of their plight. "By dawn, we must be far from the city, lest the spies of the Vizier get wind of our plan."

"Agreed," he says. The sands themselves shall cover our passage." His hand rests briefly on her shoulder, a gesture that conveys both gratitude and the promise of protection. Together, we will traverse the dunes, scale the crags, and awaken the old sorcerer from his solitude."

"Then let us hasten," Zenobia says, her figure poised like a Roc and ready to take wing. With a final glance at the sleeping city, they head for the stables to saddle their steeds.

As they work in tandem, securing waterskins and satchels, the whispered secrets of the desert night seem to rally around them, granting silent approval to the guardians of Aggrabad's destiny.

Moonlight bathes the courtyard in a silvery glow as they secure the last of their gear upon each steed. The horses, sensing the urgency of their departure, paw at the ground, their breath almost visible in the cool night air.

"The mountains are treacherous at this time of the year," he says. "We must keep a steady pace but not exhaust the horses just in case we face unexpected trials."

Zenobia nods in agreement, as she ties a bundle of supplies to her saddlebag. "Fear not, Hakim. I have traversed these paths before. The wind and stars will guide us."

Hakim meets her gaze, conscious of the resolve in her deep brown eyes. They have shared many trials, but none as perilous as the one that lies ahead. He mounts his horse, a powerful stallion with a coat as dark as the night.

"Then let us ride with the swiftness of the desert wind," he declares, his voice barely above a whisper, and one that carries the weight of their mission.

Zenobia swings herself onto the mare, a creature as graceful and fierce as she is, and with a fluid motion, she gathers the reins, and her mount responds with an eager snort. Within minutes, they leave the stables far behind.

The hooves of the horses are muffled by the soft sand that carpets the city. As they venture deeper into the desert, they are venturing into unknown territory, a realm of ancient magic and untold dangers.

The gleaming spires of the city are now far behind, the comforting sounds of their limestone oasis has faded away, only to be replaced by the vast silence of the desert. The air is crisp, and a chill in the air hints at the approach of dawn, but the sun's first rays are hours away.

The journey takes them past a deserted rock fortress, where shadows keep watch over the empty halls of the kings of old. They ride swiftly, aware that the Vizier's agents are as numerous as the grains of sand beneath their feet.

"Keep your eyes sharp," Hakim cautions as he scans the horizon for any sign of pursuit. "The Vizier's reach is long and his minions are unyielding."

"Let them come," Zenobia replies, her voice laced with defiance. "We will show them the strength of those who fight for justice."

With every mile they cover, the city becomes a distant dream, a jewel shrouded by the night. Ahead lies the open desert, its vastness both a mantle of secrecy and a daunting expanse they must cross.

Hakim feels the familiar weight of responsibility settle upon his shoulders, heavier than his armour or the weapons at his side. Yet beside him rides Zenobia, her presence a talisman against despair.

"Aggrabad shall not fall while we draw breath," he vows. His words are not just a promise to Zenobia but an oath to the city that gave birth to him.

"Nor on our watch," Zenobia says, her silhouette merging with the darkness as if she were part of the night and its master.

They spur the horses onwards, and the animals respond with renewed vigor, travelling over dunes and through valleys they ride, the stars, their silent guides.

As the landscape yields to their relentless passage, Hakim allows himself to believe that hope is more than a fleeting shadow in the desert, that it is something real, and something worth fighting for. And fight they will until the sands themselves bear witness to their victory or their valorous end.

CHAPTER 9

Hakim spreads out a map, most of which is the expanse of the vast golden desert. A few jagged lines represent mountain ranges but other symbols speak of hidden dangers and long-forgotten paths.

"The water skins are full and the food is packed away," Zenobia says as she places dates, dried lamb, and barley cakes in a leather satchel, along with a few exotic spices, a scent which mingles briefly with the evening air.

"Excellent," Hakim says, his voice steady as he folds the delicate paper carefully and tucks it behind his burnished armor. 'But how will we have to find our way through this endless desert."

"This could be useful," Zenobia says as she hands him a small metal disc inscribed with a pattern of lines.

"It's an astrolabe, an instrument that can identify the stars in the sky, and it will come in very useful, especially if we decide to travel at night."

"That will be very useful indeed. Thank you," Hakim says as his hand briefly touches hers, a silent token of gratitude for the bond they share. Together, they have faced sorcerers and demons alike, and a perilous journey like this will not test their unbreakable alliance.

As twilight approaches, it casts elongated shadows across the vast and immeasurable desert. This is a place of both beauty and danger, and a reminder that they are leaving behind a place of desert flowers and flowing water, one which is threatened by the very darkness they seek to vanquish.

"Nightfall is upon us. We must move swiftly and avoid the Vizier's sentinels," Hakim says, his green eyes reflecting the first glimmer of starlight.

Zenobia nods in agreement, her expression resolute. "Under the moon's cloak, we shall be but shadows among the dunes. The spies will search in vain."

"May the wisdom of our forebears protect us on our path," he says, as he glances up at the crescent moon rising in the indigo sky.

"May the Shadhavar sing us safe passage, and the Karkadann honor our quest with its might," Zenobia says, her voice low but filled with fervor.

"Those creatures are not always known for their sympathy or their friendliness," he says.

They exchange a look of mutual understanding and laugh for the first time in ages. Then, without another word, they shoulder their packs and step into the cool night. The stars overhead are their silent guides as they set forth on a clandestine journey, one that will take them far from the oasis city that is both their sanctuary and the wellspring of their deepest fears.

The desert rarely reveals its secrets, and neither does the night, but it may have been doing so as they make their way across the dunes. They move with the practiced stealth of warriors, each step deliberate, leaving faint trails that wash away in the breeze. Silence envelops them like a shroud, save for the soft rustle of their cloaks and the occasional cry of a desert fox.

Hakim stops and raises his hand to signal caution. Zenobia, attuned to his movements, stops as well, her senses razor-sharp. They feel it before they see it, a sinister chill that creeps up their spine and slithers into their consciousness. A low growl, a rumble in the stillness, a sound that no resident of the desert could ever make.

"Demons," Hakim says, his voice barely a whisper but laden with dread. He locks eyes with Zenobia, his gaze conveying an urgency that needs no words.

She peers into the darkness, her pulse quickening as she discerns the ghastly shapes materializing in the distance. The Vizier's sorcery has conjured up an adversary of the worst kind.

"Nasnas," she says, " only a wizard is capable of conjuring such creatures."

Nasnas are abominations that bear no resemblance to the creatures of the natural world. Their features are twisted and exaggerated, an unsettling mockery of a human being.

Their limbs are elongated beyond nature's intention, their fingers are talons meant for rending flesh, and their fractured mouth is full of needle-like teeth.

Hakim's eyes are narrow as he watches a Nasnas shift its shape and transform from a benign desert hare into a caricature of a human being, its glowing eyes locking onto its prey with predatory anticipation.

"They are bred to deceive," he says as he tightens the grip on his sword, knowing well the cunning that these shapeshifters wield.

He readies himself, his senses sharp, aware that these demons will test more than just their physical prowess; they will assail their very senses.

The air quivers with a malign presence as the Nasnas circle them from all sides, making snake-like noises that seem to come from everywhere.

"Can you trust what you see, Hakim?" one of the Nasnas says, its voice a malevolent melody designed to creep into the mind like a serpent in the sand.

"Or perhaps your eyes deceive you," another says, as it shifts its shape from a jackal to an imitation of Hakim himself.

Zenobia's eyes are fixed on this horde of half-seen shadows. "They cannot break us with illusions," she says.

"Move as far back as you can," he says. "I will send these creatures back to where they belong."

It is thanks to the legacy of his forebears and the generosity of a sorcerer from a time long past that Hakim has a power which he rarely ever uses.

"Your tricks will not avail you against the light of truth," he cries.

He closes his eyes and transforms himself into the demon god of fire, an electrically charged creature with an overabundance of atomically charged arms that glow like red hot pokers.

He exposes one energetic talon after another and envelops the Nasnas in a web of blistering hot flames. They recoil in pain and agony and dive deep into the sand dunes, never to be seen again.

"That worked," he says.

They barely have time to take a breath before the ground beneath their feet begins to tremble. A new adversary is approaching, one with the power to make the very earth shudder in fear.

"Quickly, through the pass," Zenobia cries, her melodic tone now laced with an edge of concern.

They head for the gaping maw of the mountain, a narrow ravine and the only route that promises some semblance of shelter from their pursuers. The path winds ever upwards, a serpentine trail flanked by jagged rocks that reach out like the fingers of a giant.

Their chests heave as they push their bodies to the limit. Hakim's muscular frame, once a bastion of strength, now feels the strain of the relentless pace. Zenobia's keen eyes scan the treacherous terrain, her mind calculating each twist and turn even as her heart races with fear.

They crawl under low-hanging ledges and leap over chasms that threaten to swallow them into oblivion. And with each step, the sound of their pursuers grows louder, a cacophony of malice that echoes off the walls of the pass. Their pursuers loom ever closer, a palpable force bearing down upon the two fugitives.

"Stay close," Hakim cries, his deep voice cutting through the night.

Zenobia's feet hardly touch the ground as she matches Hakim's every step, her lithe form slipping through the mountain tracks with the grace of a desert wind. Her thoughts are a whirlwind of strategy and concern, not just for her safety but also for Hakim's.

The mountain pass never seems to end. Its craggy jaws threaten to clamp down upon them at every turn, but they cannot afford to stop; their pursuer probably has an insatiable hunger.

They press on, their hearts pounding in unison against the specter of capture. Ahead, the mountain pass starts to widen, offering a sliver of hope, a promise that they might escape the clutches of the Vizier's vile minions.

The path leads to a precipice and beyond that the earth drops into an abyss of darkness. Zenobia grabs Hakim by the arm and they come to a dead halt.

"By the stars, it ends here," she cries, her eyes searches for salvation but there isn't any.

"Not yet, it doesn't," he says, his voice a bastion of resolve. His rarely-used range of skills are hereditary, passed down over time, a gift of an ancient sorcerer, and Hakim is about to be put them to good use.

He holds out his hands, words of power spill from his lips in a language older than the desert itself, and the air trembles with anticipation.

Zenobia watches, awe-struck, as the ground rumbles beneath them. Stones rise from the bottom of the chasm and assemble into a familiar form at Hakim's silent command. A broad and sturdy bridge suspended over nothingness now spans the divide, a product of Hakim's indomitable will.

"Quickly!" he cries as he grabs her hand. They race across the fragile ribbon of stone that sways slightly under their weight. And when they reach the other side, they look back just in time to see it crumbling away, leaving no trace of their passage.

Their respite is brief, but the chilling howls of the bloodthirsty Nasnas are somewhere close by and getting closer with every passing minute. Zenobia's heart thunders in her ears, an erratic drumbeat that spurs them onwards. Hakim's breath is ragged but unwavering; even as his body screams for rest, his spirit is unyielding.

"Let's go through the valley; we may lose them in the dunes," Zenobia says. Her knowledge of the land is their only guide in the moon's meager light. They descend into the valley, their feet slipping on the loose sand as they push themselves beyond the brink of exhaustion.

"Those demons are still on our tail," he says. "We have to keep moving."

Zenobia's steps never falter, and her determination matches Hakim's stride for stride. They follow a path through treacherous terrain, all the while indifferent to the gaze of the constellations watching from above.

They finally emerge from the shadowy embrace of the mountain pass into the vast expanse of the desert, where the heat of the sun is relentless.

The ground beneath their weary feet is no longer jagged stone but an endless blanket of scorching sand. The air shivers with heat, and the horizon shimmers like a mirage, taunting them with its unattainable distance.

"Zenobia," Hakim says, his voice dry as parchment, "we cannot survive this crossing unaided."

She nods knowingly, her eyes squinting against the glare. "The Vizier's demons may fear daylight, but the desert is a demon of another kind."

Hakim closes his eyes and reaches into the nascent wellspring of magic that bubbles in his soul. He extends his arms with palms facing the unforgiving sky. Words older than the shifting sands emerge from his lips, a language born from the earth's core.

And then, a shimmering veil of light materialises above them, an ethereal canopy that ripples with hues of emerald and gold. It stretches wide and casts a cool shadow to protect them from the blistering heat.

"By the grace of the ancients," Zenobia cries, her relief palpable as she steps under the protective dome.

"Let us not tarry," Hakim says as he adjusts the straps of his pack. "This magic will hold, but it drains my strength with every step we take."

Onward, they trek, and the sand whispers secrets of ancient times, but the shield holds steadfast, a bubble of reprieve amidst the inferno of the desert. Yet their bodies bear the weight of exhaustion, and the thirst for respite gnaws at their resolve.

As the sun reaches its zenith, spelling doom for any mortal caught unprotected in its reign, fate offers a rare kindness. To their relief, they see a glimmer of verdant green on the horizon.

"An oasis," Zenobia exclaims, her voice tinged with relief. Nestled between two dunes is a haven, an impossible jewel in the barrenness of this wasteland.

They hasten towards salvation, and the glistening veil above their heads follows along like the train of a spectral cloak. As they draw closer, they hear the familiar sounds of life, a symphony of trickling water, rustling palm fronds, and the call of hidden birds to welcome them into its sweet embrace.

"Alhamdulillah, praise be to God," Hakim says as he thanks the heavens and allows the magical shield to dissipate.

Date palms stand sentinel around a pool of crystalline water, and even the air is perfumed with the scent of oleander and jasmine, a stark contrast to the arid breath of the surrounding desert.

They kneel by the water's edge, scoop the life-giving liquid into their mouth with cupped hands, and drink deeply, replenishing their parched spirits before refilling the waterskins.

"Rest now," Hakim says, his green eyes reflecting the tranquil waters. "We can only afford to stay for a short while, but it shall be enough to strengthen our hearts for the journey ahead."

They find a spot beneath the shade of a generous tree and share a meal of dates and flatbread, allowing their bodies a moment of peace. In the silence, there is an unspoken understanding: the oasis is but a fleeting sanctuary, and their quest for the Cave of the Ancients will brook no delay.

With their supplies replenished and their resolve fortified, they leave the refuge that soothed their weary souls. They cast one last glance at the peaceful waterhole and carry the memory of the oasis as a talisman against the trials that await beyond the border of that sanctuary.

Hakim takes the lead, his senses sharpened by the perilous journey ahead. The desert sands shift beneath their feet, a tapestry of gold and amber stretching endlessly into the horizon. But it is not the barren beauty that command his attention, it is the sound of magic, a sinister hum that vibrates through the air.

"Be careful," he says as he halts Zenobia's advance. His eyes narrow as he scans the dunes for signs of disturbance and notices something unusual. "It's a network of traps laid by the Vizier," Hakim says.

He murmurs an incantation, one that is known only to the most adept of sorcerers. A soft glow emanates from his fingertips, only to reveal the outline of arcane symbols etched into the sand.

With deft movements, he traces new patterns in the air and counters each magical snare with ease. The traps dissipate one by one and unravel like threads pulled from a tapestry until nothing remains but harmless sand.

"Your instincts are as sharp as ever," Zenobia says, her eyes reflecting admiration and relief.

"Let us not tarry," he says, though a hint of pride colours his tone. "We must press on."

Zenobia nods in agreement, her gaze lifting to the vast expanse above, and with a grace born of both human and avian, her transformation begins. Her limbs lengthen, feathers sprout and unfurl, her body contorts, and then she shrinks into the lithe form of a falcon. In mere moments, where once stood a woman, there is now a majestic bird, its golden wings catching the sunlight.

She launches herself into the sky with a powerful beat of her wings, ascending higher and higher until she is but a speck against the canvas of the azure sky. From her vantage point above, she surveys the landscape with the keen eyes of a raptor searching for any sign of the Vizier's minions or any other danger hidden amongst the dunes and rocky outcrops.

Below, Hakim watches her ascent, a surge of protectiveness warms his heart as he admires her strength and the sheer force of her will. Together, they are an indomitable force, but he steels himself for whatever trials they must face next in this unforgiving land.

As Zenobia circles above, the wind carries her hawkish cry back to Hakim, a signal that the path ahead is clear for now. With a determined stride, he carries on, knowing that while the skies are watched by Zenobia's vigilant eyes, the earth below will be safeguarded by his own unwavering resolve.

Sand whips across the barren landscape, a scourge born from the depths of the Rub al-Khali's fury. Hakim shields his eyes from the maelstrom that seeks to devour them whole. Zenobia returns to her human form and takes his hand, her fingers a vice of determination.

"Stay close," he says, his voice barely audible over the howling winds. They trudge onwards, each step a monumental effort as the dunes shift beneath their feet.

The air is a blur of swirling grains and relentless gusts, but they press on, leaning into the storm that rages like a djinn awakened in wrath. Their silhouettes are ephemeral ghosts dancing on the edge of oblivion, yet neither falters. Hakim's heart is pounding, not solely from exertion but with the drive to protect, serve, and endure.

"Look," Zenobia cries, "there in the distance. That's it."

An ancient structure emerges from the swirling sands. Its time-worn stones stand defiant against the eons. A temple, half-buried and forgotten, whispers secrets within its hallowed halls.

As they approach, a colossal figure materialises from the chaos. It's a sphinx, regal, menacing, and magnificent that sees all, an ancient intelligence lurking in its unfathomable feline eyes.

"Who dares seek entry to this sacred place?" it says, its voice a rumble that melds with the storm's fury.

Hakim steps forward and says, "I am Hakim Al-Rashid, Captain of the Guards of Aggrabad, and this is Zenobia al-Farsi. We seek passage to fulfill a quest of great importance."

"Many have sought, and few have passed," the sphinx says. "Answer my riddle, and the path shall open. Fail and be forever lost amidst the sands."

"Ask your riddle, noble guardian," Hakim says, his green eyes unwavering.

"Lighter than a feather, yet no man can hold it for long. What am I?"

Silence hangs like a thread on the wind, and the weight of their fate balances on the tip of his tongue. Zenobia's grip tightens a silent plea. "Breath," Hakim replies, his voice as steady as a mountain rock.

The air vibrates as the sphinx inclines its head, and the storm subsides to a mere whisper. "Pass, travelers of valor and wisdom."

With a nod of gratitude, they cross the threshold. The heavy stone doors of the temple grind open to welcome them into the dim coolness of its ancient corridors. Behind them, the howl of the sandstorm fades as if the desert bows to the will of those who have earned the right to unveil its mysteries.

They head deeper into the temple, their boots echoing on the stone floor, a rhythmic counterpoint to their quickened pulse. They move with purpose, their torches casting long shadows that dance upon walls inscribed with tales of gods and mortals locked in an epic struggle. The air is heavy with the scent of ancient incense and dust, a testament to centuries undisturbed.

"Here," Zenobia says as she directs his gaze to an ornate archway veiled by a tapestry woven with threads of silver and gold. With a shared nod, they approach and move the fabric aside to reveal a chamber untouched by time.

Inside are artifacts of silent splendor: jeweled chalices, carved ivory statuettes, and bronze lamps shaped like serpents. Scrolls of papyrus and vellum are carefully stacked on wooden shelves, their bindings embossed with lapis lazuli and carnelian.

Hakim's fingers brush over the scrolls, each a fragile relic eager to divulge its secrets. "We must find the map," he says, as he scans each of the texts with eyes honed by years of tactical study. His heart thrums with anticipation; every artifact holds the wisdom of the ancients and, among them, their key to their salvation.

"Look for the seal of the Cave," he says, his voice barely louder than the hush of shifting sand beyond the temple walls.

Hakim notices a scroll sealed with wax. The emblem is a crescent moon cradling a star. Carefully breaking the seal, he unfurls the parchment, only to discover a detailed map marked with constellations and cryptic symbols that chart a path through the desert to the fabled Cave of the Ancients.

"By the ancestors, we have found it," Hakim cries, his relief mingling with the thrill of discovery.

However, their moment of triumph is short-lived as the ground starts to tremble beneath their feet. Dust cascades from the ceiling, and a distant, ominous rumble reaches their ears. They exchange a look of understanding; time is now their most relentless pursuer.

With the map secure in his satchel, Hakim leads the way out of the chamber. Their steps hasten as the temple groans in protest at this intrusion. The exit looms ahead, promising freedom and fresh danger.

The sun blazes outside, a stark contrast to the cool darkness within. They step back into the relentless heat, but Hakim's concern is not for the sun's wrath. Before them is a vast ravine, its depths lost in shadow, a formidable sentinel that bars their way.

"Magic is our ally on this day," he says as he taps into the wellspring of power within. He extends his hands, palms facing the abyss, and with a deep incantation, he summons his will.

The earth answers his call, and the stones shift and rise and coalesce into a solid structure. A bridge of rock gracefully arches across the chasm, one that defies gravity and expectation.

"Quickly, Zenobia," he says as they head for the bridge, faithfully trusting in his magic to hold.

They cross with swift strides, and the bridge holds firm beneath their weight. As soon as they reach the other side, Hakim allows the spell to dissipate, and the bridge crumbles and falls into the darkness below.

"Forward lies our destiny," he says. With the map to guide them and their resolve as their shield, they turn their backs on the abyss and make for the horizon, where the Cave of the Ancients awaits.

The sun dips below the horizon, casting its last rays upon a weary but resolute pair. Hakim's boots crunch upon the gravelly soil, his cloak is covered in the dust of countless miles. Zenobia moves silently by his side, her brown eyes survey the landscape with the acuity of an eagle.

The Cave of the Ancients looms before them, a gaping mouth set into the face of an ancient cliff, veiled in shadows that whisper of secrets untold.

"We're almost there," Hakim says, his deep voice carrying an undercurrent of fatigue that he can no longer conceal. His olive brown skin is drawn tight over high cheekbones, a testament to an arduous journey.

He holds the leather satchel containing their precious supplies close to his chest, as well as the map that led them here. Their once-hearty provisions now feel like leaden weights at his side.

"Abdullah awaits," Zenobia says. "Our hope lies with him and that cave."

With each step, Hakim feels the pull of destiny tugging at his heart, a force as tangible as the scabbard at his side. He recalls the tales of a man of miracles, Abdullah al-Hakim, the sorcerer whose wisdom once shaped nations and whose power defied even time itself. This is the man they seek; Abdullah is the key to saving Aggrabad from the Vizier's dark machinations.

As they approach the threshold, the air grows cooler, and the oppressive heat of the desert begins to retreat like a defeated enemy. Hakim's eyes, usually so clear with purpose, now flicker with uncertainty. What lies ahead is unknown territory, even for one such as he, who was raised on the legends of old.

"Remember, Hakim," Zenobia says, "magic is more than just the elements. It is borne of courage, of the will to stand against the darkness."

Her words fortify his resolve and fills his heart with hopefulness. Not long after, they notice the faint glow of a crystal in the distance, one that pulses with an otherworldly light. It beckons them forward, promising sanctuary and knowledge.

"That is the entrance to the cave," Hakim says, his voice regaining its usual timbre of authority.

They cross the final stretch, their shadows elongated across the rocky ground. At the mouth of the cave, they pause, and allow themselves a moment to take in the gravity of what they are about to do. To seek out Abdullah is to step into legend, to intertwine their fates with a force beyond mortal ken.

They summon their last vestige of strength and step across the ancient threshold, and into the cool of the darkness that envelops them like a shroud. The world of sand and sky melts away, only to be replaced by the silence of the Cave of the Ancients. A faint light that emanates from Abdullah's staff beckons them to go deeper into the heart of the mountain, towards the wisdom that might yet save their city.

"Abdullah," Hakim cries out hopefully, "we have come."

The sound of his voice reminds Hakim that he is a Captain of the Guards, a protector, and a beacon of hope. With Zenobia at his side, he is ready to face whatever trials await him for Aggrabad, for justice, and for the future they dare to dream.

CHAPTER 10

After many undisturbed centuries, the air in the Cave of the Ancients still carries the weight of profound mystery. Shadows cling to the walls like ancient guardians, whispering secrets of a time long past.

Hakim's olive skin takes on the pallor of the dimly lit cavern, and his broad frame casts a formidable silhouette against the flickering light from their torch.

Zenobia follows closely behind, her once vibrant gown now dull with the dust of their travels. She scans the recesses of the cave with an alertness that belies her exhaustion. They have traversed the unforgiving Rub al-Khali Desert and evaded the cunning Nasnas, and now, in the heart of the mountain, the final leg of their quest lays before them.

The air grows denser as they move deeper into the cave, the subtle scent of ancient incense lingering like a ghost. They finally arrive at a chamber where time seems to stand still, and there, upon a bed crafted of woven reeds is Abdullah al-Hakim, the sorcerer whose reputation for wisdom transcends the boundaries of ages.

Abdullah's chest rises and falls with the faintest rhythm of life, each breath a shallow testament to his enduring spirit. His white beard flows over the edge of the bed like a river of time. His piercing blue eyes, which have seen the rise and fall of empires, are now fixed upon Hakim with a clarity that cuts through the shadows.

"Abdullah," Hakim cries, the reverence in his voice echoing softly through the cavernous space. The old sorcerer's gaze holds him and conveys a depth of knowledge and understanding that words can never fully express. In that moment, Hakim realizes that an ancient lineage of guardianship which stretches back generations now rests upon his shoulders.

Zenobia stands silently by his side, her presence a comforting constant. She watches the exchange between the two men, aware of the profound significance of what is to come. Together, they have faced countless dangers, but this silent communion bears a gravity that transcends any battle they have ever fought.

As Hakim meets Abdullah's gaze, he is all too aware that the weight of Aggrabad's fate hovers on the brink, and his actions, guided by the wisdom of the ancients will tip the scales.

The Cave of the Ancients, with its timeless echo, has borne witness to countless moments, and now it watches closely and is ready to record the outcome of another pivotal chapter in the saga of their world.

Hakim steps forward, the coarse fabric of his travel-worn cloak brushing against the cold stone floor. The rhythm of his heart matches the distant throbbing of ancient drums in his ears, a sound heard only by those who stand on the precipice of destiny.

He extends his hand, calloused from the hilt of his sword and the reins of his steed, and gently clasps the almost ethereal fingers of Abdullah.

"Master," he says, a storm of emotions swirling within as he touches the sorcerer's paper thin hands, both of which are slowly losing their power.

Abdullah's eyes are not unlike the deep blue of the ocean or even the eternal sky. With an effort that contorts his serene face, he draws a breath that fills the silence of the cave.

"Child of Aggrabad," he says, each word resonating in Hakim's soul, "darkness gathers upon our land like a tempest born from the very depths of the abyss."

His voice is but a whisper and Hakim has to lean closer, his senses sharpening so that he can capture every fleeting syllable.

"Aggrabad, the jewel of the desert, stands upon the edge of annihilation," Abdullah says, his gaze piercing the very fabric of Hakim's being. "The city calls for a guardian, a protector whose heart beats in unison with its ancient stones."

Hakim is aware that a solemn duty is about to settle on his shoulders like a mantle heavier than any armor that he has ever donned before.

Aggrabad, with its ivory spires and verdant oasis, is more than his home; it is a legacy entrusted to his care, a sacred trust passed down through a bloodline of warriors.

"Your lineage has prepared you for this burden, Hakim Al-Rashid," the sorcerer says, his fingers tightening around Hakim's. "And the time has come for you to rise and protect the Atlantis of the Desert from the storm that seeks to erase its memory from the world."

As the words wash over him, Hakim is aware that the very fabric of his reality is shifting. The responsibility that now falls upon his shoulders is beyond the comprehension of ordinary men, but he is no ordinary man. He is the Captain of the Guards, bred for valor and forged in the fires of honor. It is his destiny to stand as a bulwark against the coming darkness, to hold the line where others would falter.

Abdullah's grip relaxes; his message has been imparted, and at that moment, Hakim stands at the threshold of fate, ready to embrace the path that destiny has carved out for him.

Clutching the aged hand of the sorcerer, he finds his voice amidst the silence that shrouds the Cave.

"By my life and my blade," he says, the words quivering as they escape his lips, betraying the tempest in his soul. His grip tightens, not out of desperation, but to fortify the oath that pours from his heart. "I swear to protect Aggrabad and its people.

"As long as breath fills my chest and blood flows in my veins, I shall stand as the shield against the darkness." Determination ignites like a beacon in his emerald eyes and reflects an unyielding resolve that rivals the desert sun.

Abdullah's pale blue eyes hold him for a moment longer, an unspoken acknowledgment passing between them. Then, with an effort that draws upon the last wells of his strength, the sorcerer releases Hakim's hand and raises his own toward the heavens. The air in the cave grows heavy as if charged with an invisible current, and Abdullah's lips part to utter words that were ancient, even when the world was young.

"Strength for he who is the First," Abdullah says, his voice echoes through the cave, each syllable a resonant thrum that vibrates along the stone walls and into the very bones of those who stand as a witness.

The language of this mystical ceremony is one forgotten by time, known only to those who commune with the ethereal and the divine. Abdullah's incantations rises and falls in a haunting cadence, summoning powers that have slumbered in the shadows of the world.

Hakim is rooted to the spot, the weight of his new purpose coalescing with the words that dance through the cavern. Each intonation seems to peel back the layers of reality, revealing glimpses of the arcane forces that Abdullah commands, forces that will soon become Hakim's to wield.

A soft glow emanates from Abdullah's staff, casting prismatic light across the chamber, illuminating the ancient symbols etched into the rock and setting them aglow with an otherworldly energy.

The old sorcerer's voice intertwines with the essence of the cave itself, almost as though the very fabric of the universe is bending to his will, acknowledging the gravity of the covenant being forged.

Hakim stands tall, anchored by his devotion to Aggrabad. He is ready to embrace the mantle of protector to become the avatar of an age-old legacy that has chosen him to rise in its defense.

As Abdullah's ancient hand touches his, an electric current travels up Hakim's arm, a river of warmth that floods his entire being with an indescribable energy.

His muscles quiver, not with exhaustion but with a burgeoning power that pulses in rhythmic waves. And each beat of his heart synchronizes with the hum of magic now awakening in his veins.

Once still and heavy with the weight of imminent peril, the cave vibrates with an unseen force as if it recognizes the significance of the transference.

Hakim's olive skin shimmers in the dim light, illuminating the transformation taking root in his soul. His green eyes, which have always been a wellspring of strength, now glint with an inner fire that speaks of ancient mysteries unraveling their secrets for him alone.

Zenobia stands motionless; she sees the man she knows and the powerful sorcerer he will become. She is a witness to his subtle transformation, the imperceptible straightening of his spine, as though invisible strings are pulling him upwards to meet his destiny. Her hands itch to reach out, to touch the magic that embraces this man, yet she remains still, her respect for the ritual paramount.

Zenobia's presence is a beacon of support, and her loyalty and courage are as palpable as Hakim's newfound power. There is wonder in her gaze but also a recognition of the path that they walk. Her destiny is entwined with his, and her abilities are linked to their success or failure. A silent vow echoes through the chamber, an unspoken promise that whatever challenges lay ahead, they will face them together.

As Abdullah continues to channel his powers into Hakim's soul, the air is charged with anticipation and the echoes of a thousand ancient battles. At this moment, Hakim is all too aware of the lineage of his forebears, the valiant warriors of Aggrabad, who stand sentinel but unseen. He is the nexus of their hopes, the vessel of their undying spirit, ready to rise against the encroaching darkness with Zenobia, his steadfast ally, at his side.

The very air of the Cave of the Ancients vibrates with the crescendo of Abdullah's incantations, a symphony of power that summons the essence of the universe itself. Every syllable resonates within the core of Hakim's being, an ancient language that is both alien and intimately known to his soul.

A moment later, the shadows in the cave retreat as if cowering from an unseen light. Then, without warning, a brilliance bursts forth and envelops everything. It is as if the Sun had been plucked from the sky and is nestling within the heart of the cave. The ancient symbols carved into the limestone walls come alive, pulsing with luminescence, their meanings imparting silent wisdom to all who behold them.

Hakim stands at the center of this maelstrom, his body a conduit for the blinding radiance that pours from Abdullah's outstretched hands. The once-dim recesses of the cave now dance with silhouettes that leap and twirl across the walls, a tapestry of light and darkness that plays out the story of ages past.

As quickly as it had flared, the light begins to dim, and the cave returns to a serene gloom. But a very different glow now emanates from Hakim. He looks taller, his chest expands with each breath, and his olive skin basks in an ethereal luminescence that seems to stem from deep within.

His eyes, those piercing green orbs, now shimmer with an inner flame. They hold the spark of newfound magic, a reflection of the profound gift that Abdullah has bestowed upon him. It is not just light that shines from Hakim's gaze but determination, a resolute promise to wield this power in defense of Aggrabad and its people.

The ceremony has reached its zenith, and all that remains is a silence that speaks volumes. Hakim Al-Rashid, Captain of the Guards, is now more than a mere man, he is now a bastion of hope, armored in the ancient magic of his ancestors, ready to face whatever darkness threatens his beloved city.

Abdullah's chest rises and falls once more, and his eyes, now the color of winter skies are locked onto Hakim's in a gaze that transcends the physical. With his final breath, one as soft as a desert breeze, the old sorcerer releases himself from his mortal coil and ascends beyond the vaulted ceilings carved by time itself.

"Go well into the night, wise one," Hakim says, his voice barely audible over the hum of residual magic in the air.

The silence that follows is profound, punctuated only by the drip of ancient groundwater. Zenobia bows reverently at the passing of a soul older than the sands of time. The chamber feels different now and a little emptier, as if Abdullah's departure has taken more than just his spirit, it has taken someone who has stood his ground for longer than they know.

The power that courses through Hakim's body is immense, a raging river of potential that threatens to overwhelm his senses. He can feel it beneath his skin, between each heartbeat, a force that is both exhilarating and terrifying.

His mind races with visions of Aggrabad's white limestone walls, its bustling marketplaces filled with the scent of spices and the sound of laughter. He sees the faces of those who look up to him, those who call him protector, and those who know nothing of the doom that creeps along like a thief in the night.

He opens his eyes, and for a moment, he is back in the city he loves, standing at the gates as Captain of the Guards. But the illusion changes when he notices the ancient symbols on the cave walls, their meanings all too clear now. They speak of battles fought, of lives saved, of sacrifices made, all of which are woven into the fabric of legends long before his time.

Determination sets his jaw and resolve steels his spine. He is Hakim Al-Rashid, scion of warriors, chosen by prophecy. His legacy will not be one of defeat. Aggrabad's fate rests on his shoulders, and he will bear it with the honor of his forebears.

"Zenobia," he says, his voice steady yet filled with the gravity of their quest. "We must return. The city needs us."

She nods, silent but resolute, a testament to the bond they share, a bond now sealed by destiny. Together, they will face the unknown, their wills united against the shadows that seek to claim their home.

The silence in the Cave of the Ancients is profound and a witness to the monumental shift that has taken place. Hakim's hands are clenched at his sides, a raw power courses through his veins like a river breaking free from an ancient dam. As he stands amidst the echoes of Abdullah's last breath, a weight presses upon his chest, a responsibility so vast that it threatens to crush him.

Zenobia taps him on the shoulder and arouses him from his reverie. Her touch is as light as a feather but carries the strength of steel. Her hand is warm against his skin, her presence a balm to the tumult in his heart. He turns to her, and in the soft glow that lingers in the cave, he sees not just a warrior and ally but a beacon of hope, a symbol for everyone in Aggrabad.

"Remember, we are not alone," she says, her voice a melody amid the cacophony of his thoughts. "Your bravery and my wings will carry us through the storm."

Hakim draws a deep breath; the scent of the ancient stones and the lingering magic fills his lungs. Her words remind him of their unity, how her strength complements his own. Even the weight of prophecies can be borne with her by his side.

With a nod, he acknowledges the truth in her words. Their combined might is Aggrabad's shield; together, they will stand firm against the creeping darkness. The burden of leadership has eased ever so slightly. Still, he knows that Zenobia's wisdom will guide them when the path grows uncertain.

He makes a silent promise of protection to the city that gave birth to him and the people who trust him. But now, it's time to leave the sanctum that holds the remnants of ancient sorcery and return to the world of sand and sun.

"Let us go," he says, his tone imbued with a newfound resolve. "Aggrabad awaits, and our destiny is not one of surrender."

Zenobia withdraws her hand, only to offer it anew, palm up and open, an invitation to join forces in every step they will take. He accepts; his grip is firm, and it seals their pact without words.

They gather their sparse belongings, the artifacts of their journey now infused with the weight of prophecy. Each item finds its place in their packs; each placement is a testament to their readiness to face what lies ahead.

As they move towards the entrance of the cave, their shadows dance on the walls, intermingling as if to mimic the union of their spirits. Hakim's armor clinks softly, a song of resilience, while Zenobia's cloak whispers tales of flight and freedom.

Steps sure, eyes bright with purpose, Hakim and Zenobia traverse the cave's threshold. The chill of the cavern gives way to the warmth of anticipation, and their hearts beat to the rhythm of a single, unyielding drum, the heartbeat of Aggrabad itself.

A blinding light greets their eyes as they breach the mouth of the Cave. It's a stark contrast to the dim glow of the enchanted stones that illuminated their subterranean vigil. Hakim shields his gaze for a moment, and allows his vision to adjust, while the desert's heat envelops him like a familiar old cloak.

Zenobia squints against the glare of the midday sun. The expanse before them stretches vast and unyielding; dunes rise and fall like waves on a golden sea, and the limestone structures of Aggrabad shimmer like a mirage in their mind.

They pause at the threshold between shadow and light, the silence speaking volumes of the journey ahead. Hakim can feel the weight of Abdullah's prophecy settling upon his shoulders, a mantle he is destined to wear, yet one that feels as tangible as his armour.

Zenobia turns her gaze upon Hakim. Her deep brown eyes reflect the fiery determination that now stirs within him. Her hand finds his, not in need but as equals, partners whose fate is entwined with the survival of their beloved city. Their fingers intertwine, a silent promise that neither will have to face the darkness alone.

That unspoken conversation speaks of battles to come, of unseen enemies, and of the steadfast courage required to overcome them. It whispers of the trust they place in each other, a bond forged through trials by fire and sanctified by ancient magic.

The air around them seems to thrum with energy, charged with the echo of Abdullah's incantations. The power coursing through Hakim's veins is a vibrant current that surges with each beat of his heart. Zenobia holds herself with the grace of one who also harbors celestial power beneath her mortal guise.

They step forward, and each footprint in the sand marks the beginning of an epic tale that is yet to unfold. The sun casts long shadows behind them, heralding the legends that will be sung of their valor.

As they descend from the cave's entrance, the arid breeze carries the faintest hint of spice and blooming flowers; the essence of Aggrabad is calling them home. With every step, they move as one, their resolve unshaken, their spirits alight with the fires of destiny.

And so, they begin their descent from the cradle of mysticism, down toward the sand dunes that will test the very limits of their strength and will. Together, they will stand against the tides of chaos, united by purpose and fortified by the love of their city. The trials ahead will be many, but Hakim and Zenobia will face them undaunted, their alliance unbreakable under the sun's unwavering gaze.

CHAPTER 11

Before they have even reached the top of the first dune, they realize that trouble is brewing. Arrayed on the top of a distant dune is a herd of Karkadann. These creatures are the fiercest of all unicorns, beings of legend, their ivory coats shimmering like a mirage in the sun, and at this moment, they are prancing on the hot dunes and ready to engage in a deadly ballet.

The horn of the beast is impossible to ignore, a spiral lance with a sinister sheen and a venomous potency. It spirals towards the heavens, catches the light, and scatters it with prismatic brilliance.

"Contact with that horn means certain death," Hakim says. "That creature is as ancient as the desert itself."

The Karkadann towers over them by half, their thick, leathery hide constantly shifting like the armored plates of a primordial behemoth.

"By the ancients," Zenobia cries. "That one at the front is massive. It could fell an army."

"We must draw it away from the others," Hakim says as he eyes its venomous horn. "A transformation could be the solution."

"I believe that they have a weakness for a beautiful woman."

"I will do my best," Zenobia says.

She closes her eyes and summons a very different sort of bird this time, and a few moments later, she transforms herself into an enchanting maiden dressed in a diaphanous gown and veil.

"Very captivating," Hakim says. "But I think you have attracted their attention already."

The eyes of the king of beasts are fixed upon Zenobia as she taunts him with a routine that any belly dancer would be proud of. It advances eagerly, entranced by a vision that appeared out of nowhere.

She obviously has a plan and leads the Karkadann on a chase of shadows and whispers. Hakim watches with interest, ready to intervene should the illusion falter, his every sense attuned to this intriguing dance of deception.

Zenobia pirouettes across the sand, a specter of grace under the relentless sun, and does her best to beguile their senses of the Karkadann and draw them as far away as possible.

The herd follows her wherever she goes, racing around in never-ending circles, but the Karkadann are programmed for one thing and one alone.

A haunting and dangerous melody, an enchantment of the worst kind, erupts from the hollows of their horns. The sound they produce is so captivating and so achingly beautiful that, after a while, it is impossible to focus on anything.

Notes weave through the air, a tapestry of sound that threatens to ensnare the mind and dull the senses. Each melody is an emotion so intense that it borders on pain, only to be followed by a profound sadness that attaches itself to the soul.

The fact that these creatures are here at all has to be a product of the Vizier's magic, but this is not music. This is a siren call to oblivion, and Hakim knows that it means peril.

He has seen strong men wander into the desert with tears streaming down their faces as they followed a Karkadann's call, never to return. He tightens his grip on his scimitar, the weapon an anchor in a sea of beguiling chords.

"Focus, Zenobia," he cries. His voice, sharp and clear, cuts through the cacophony. His words are a lifeline, pulling her back from the brink of the Karkadann's auditory abyss.

The noise fills the air and intensifies, threatening to overwhelm even Hakim's disciplined mind, and it is time to call upon forces unseen. With a deep breath that steels his resolve, he plunges his blade into the sand, and the ground trembles with an invocation.

"By the hidden fires," he cries, his voice laced with power, "I summon the King of the Djinn to my side."

The sky darkens like dusk descending prematurely on a battlefield. Whirlwinds arise from the stillness, each one a spiraling column of sand that coalesces into towering figures that rise with majestic might.

Clad in armor that gleams like polished brass, the Djinn are warriors of legend, their eyes alight with the embers of their realm. Each is a weapon unique to itself, a cosmic scimitar wreathed in flame. And as soon as they become visible, they bow reverently to their new master.

They form ranks behind Hakim, an army conjured from the very elements. And with a surge of his will, the Captain of the Guards leads them into battle, a tide of otherworldly might that crashes against the Karkadann menace.

Zenobia's voice rises above the fray, a battle cry that melds seamlessly with her transformation. In the span of a heartbeat, where once stood a woman, there is now a magnificent Roc with a wingspan that almost blocks out the Sun. Her plumage shimmers like gold, each feather etched with the wisdom of ages.

With a powerful beat of her wings, she ascends, rising above the clash of magic and horns, her keen eyes assessing the chaos below before she dives. Speed lends her form a grace that belies the strength within, and as she swoops down upon the Karkadann, her talons unsheathe, both of which are as sharp as a scimitar.

Her claws, deadly and precise strike with the force of a hammer, each blow aiming to disarm and maim. She dances through the air in a whirlwind of avian fury, her presence a formidable challenge to the mythical creatures that have been summoned by the Vizier.

Together, they are a storm of righteous vengeance, a Captain whose command over the elements matches the conviction in his heart, and a guardian whose shape can shift as readily as the winds but whose determination remains as steadfast as the mountains.

Amid the tumult of clashing forces, Hakim stands resolute. The desert winds whip around wildly as he calls forth torrents of sand to obscure the Karkadann's mesmerizing forms. Each grain seems to carry his will, a swirling barrier between innocence and enchantment. His green eyes flare with the intensity of the magic he wields, and his booming voice commands the Djinn, who rise like a tempest at his side.

"Shield your mind," he cries to his allies, the Djinn echoing his cry with their own otherworldly voices. These supernatural beings, each a marvel of elemental fury form ranks around their master, shapes blurred by the sandstorm conjured up by Hakim's mighty will.

In the sky high above, Zenobia dances on the currents of the air, her form as a Roc majestic against the backdrop of the shimmering sky. Her golden feathers glisten as though kissed by the sun itself, starkly contrasting with the battle-darkened skies. With every swoop and dive, she aims for the horns of the Karkadann, a symbol of their hypnotic power. Her movements are strategic, designed to confound and bewilder.

The battle rages, man and Djinn against beast, in a cacophony of war cries and a clash of natural and supernatural might. The Karkadann, caught in the storm of sand and feathers, fight with graceful ferocity. Their sleek bodies shine like polished ivory as they move with a dancer's precision, their horns catching the light with each elegant turn.

And it is then that they begin to sing in unison, a chorus of voices woven together in a tapestry of sound that threatens to ensnare the senses. It's a song as powerful as the desert is cruel, a haunting call from the depths of the unknown, a melody that promises serenity but delivers oblivion.

Hakim is all too aware of their power, their song is a siren's call that could beckon anyone into madness.

Yet he stands firm, his mind fortified by years of discipline and the knowledge of what is at stake. He mutters a spell under his breath, a string of ancient words that wrap around his torso like celestial armor.

"Stay strong, Zenobia," he cries, his voice a lifeline thrown across the battlefield.

Zenobia releases a piercing cry that cuts through the enchantment like a blade through silk. It's a sound that speaks of the untamed wilds, a challenge to the unnatural allure of the Karkadann. Every beat of her wings is an act of defiance, a reminder that strength lies in freedom and the fight to preserve it.

She closes her mind to the tendrils of music that seek to entwine her thoughts. In her heart, a single purpose resonates more loudly than any song ever could: to protect Aggrabad and her people at all costs.

Hakim's resolve is relentless, and each breath is an exhalation of the conjurer's art, a whirlwind that sweeps across the sands. Their enemies circle with lethal grace, their spiraling horns gleaming ominously in the moonlight.

"Zenobia, on your left," Hakim cries.

With an instinctive understanding, she banks sharply, her massive wings buffeting the air as she intercepts a charging Karkadann. Her talons lash out, striking with precision and forcing the creature to retreat. Hakim seizes the moment. His enchanted scimitar arcs through the air, and the blade hums with an energy that neutralises their hypnotic tune.

Hakim may be a novice as a sorcerer, but the art of a response is a dance that he has perfected over many conflicts. He parries and thrusts and waves his wand with a fluidity that belies his muscular frame. At the same time, Zenobia's aerial acrobatics provide both offense and defense. They are a tempest incarnate, two forces of nature bound by unwavering trust.

A cry from above attracts Hakim's attention, and he looks skyward, only to see Zenobia plummeting towards him, a glittering silhouette against the stars. His heart clenches as he realizes the danger. The songs of the Karkadann have finally reached their target, and they are waiting for her to descend.

"Watch out," he cries, his voice cracking like thunder.

Zenobia rears back in mid-descent and her wings catch the wind and alters her trajectory. Hakim summons a barrier of swirling sand to deflect a Karkadann's impending strike. Its lethal horn crashes against the gritty shield, and sparks fly in every direction as two elemental forces meet.

He is spared, but only by a hair's breadth, and the impact resonates through his body. Zenobia lands beside him, and her form reverts back to that of a human, her brown eyes meeting his with a silent nod of gratitude.

"That was close," she says, her voice steady despite the adrenaline that courses through her body.

"Too close," Hakim says, his hand finding hers briefly, reaffirming their solidarity.

They turn as one and ready themselves for the next wave of attack. The Karkadann approach with renewed vigor and weave a complex web designed to ensnare. But they stand resolute, their unity an unspoken vow to weather any storm, to survive any peril, together.

Hakim's muscles ache as he parries the effects of another spectral horn only seconds before it grazes his armor. With each clash, his resolve hardens like the steel of his blade.

"Stand firm, Hakim," Zenobia cries, her voice piercing the cacophony as she sidesteps a Karkadann intent on inflicting a significant injury.

"Remember the children's laughter in the marketplace,' she cries, "the wisdom shared in the council of the elders. Aggrabad relies on us."

Her words are a balm to his weary spirit, stoking the fires of determination that burn within. "For our home and for its people," he cries back.

They fight with a synchronicity honed by countless hours of training and battles past, their dedication forming an unbreakable bond. As the Karkadann circle once again, their haunting melodies attempt to seduce the senses, but Hakim is focused on his home and his people. They are the heartbeat that pulses through his veins, that anchors him to his resolve.

"Zenobia, your courage gives us wings," he cries as he deflects another blow, allowing her a moment to recover her stance.

"Your strength is the shield that guards the innocent," she replies, her eyes finding his amidst the chaos.

The battle rages on, a tempest of wills clashing under the desert stars. With every strike and maneuver, the Karkadann increase their determination, but Hakim and Zenobia dive into every conflict with equal determination. They will not falter, they will not fail; this they have promised each other with every breath and every heartbeat.

Hakim barely avoids yet another lethal Karkadann horn, but they keep on coming, pressing in with a ferocity that matches the desert's relentless heat. Like wraiths spun from moonlight, they charge, their spiraled horns aiming with lethal precision. Each beast is an ethereal tapestry of muscle and magic, their manes like silver waterfalls cascading over translucent skin.

"Zenobia, on your left," Hakim cries, as his voice cuts through the cacophony. The song of the Karkadann can twist the very air itself, a symphony designed to ensnare hearts and minds, but Hakim is not about to let those bewitching melodies distract him from his sacred charge.

Zenobia transforms again, and her talons slice through one creature after another, leaving deep and visible wounds, but the unicorns are relentless and as persistent as a sandstorm.

"This confrontation has to end," Hakim cries.

Drawing upon the depths of his power, he extends his arms and calls for more Djinn to come to their rescue. "Aid us, oh spirits of wind and fire," he cries, his voice deep and resonant, amplified by the force of his will.

Once again, an army of Djinn rise from the swirling sands, figures of smoke and ember. With eyes like burning coal and bodies wreathed in flame and tempest, they answer when summoned. Their presence fills the battlefield with an aura of awe-inspiring might, a counterpoint to the never-ending malevolence of the Karkadann.

"Turn their songs against them," Hakim cries.

The Djinn understands and start to weave a counter-melody, a discordant harmony that frays at the very heart of the unicorn's enchantment.

Their power is weakening and their notes are faltering under the onslaught of the Djinn, but these creatures are as ethereal as they are deadly.

Zenobia reappears and cuts through the cacophony, her talons gleaming like scimitars unsheathed for war. She strikes again and again, raking her talons across the flank of one ephemeral beast after another.

This is the moment of truth and the opportunity that Hakim needs. As his palms glow with power, he weaves an intricate symbol in the air and commands the elements to do his bidding.

The Karkadann are about to double their efforts, but the air is vibrating with such potent magic that their control wavers and their unity fractures.

Hakim orchestrates a power symbol, one that will bend the very fabric of reality to his will. And with one final guttural chant that resonates with the force of his conviction, he releases an all-encompassing command.

"By the sands and stars, he roars, "let there be silence."

That command shatters the power of the Karkadann army. The silence that follows is immediate, and their songs simply cease to exist. Their primary weapon has been rendered inert, their horns no longer shimmer with an otherworldly light, and even their eyes have lost their hypnotic glow. They are exposed and vulnerable, their power has been diminished, and the tide of battle has turned.

The Karkadann, stripped of their lethal power, rear in confusion and fear turn as one, their hooves digging into the sand as they beat a speedy retreat.

This moment, borne of courage and cunning by Hakim and Zenobia, marks the end of the Vizier's campaign, at least for the moment. They were a maelstrom of valor and might, the synergy between them unspoken but deeply felt.

"Memphalut al Shikari, Aggrabad shall not fall this day," Hakim roars, his voice slicing through the sand-filled air. "We have seen to that."

As the last beams of sunlight surrender to the twilight, a profound silence envelops the battlefield. The Karkadann have been defeated and return to the stars from whence they came.

Hakim and Zenobia stand amidst the stillness, their chests heaving, gazes locked in mutual respect and understanding. "We have prevailed against the malevolence of the Vizier once again," he cries, his spirit alight with triumph.

"Aggrabad is safe, thanks to you, Hakim Al-Rashid," Zenobia says as she returns to her human form. Her face is marked by exhaustion, yet her eyes sparkle with the tenacity that defines her.

"Thanks to us," he says as he offers her a hand to steady herself. "Together, we are the shield of this city."

They share a moment of silent communion, and their thoughts turn to the road ahead. The threat to Aggrabad is far from over; more challenges await beyond the dunes. But for now, they allow themselves a brief respite, the weight of their victory anchors them amid the shifting sands.

"Come," Hakim says, his voice firm but tinged with weariness. "The night grows cold, and our people need to know of our triumph. Our journey is far from over, but I fear that the Vizier is not finished yet."

CHAPTER 12

Before the light of a new day had even dawned, another menace conjured up by the Vizier rears its ugly head. The mythical terrors known as the Falak are demons of legend, creatures born of fire, their armour forged in the belly of a sunless forge. Their eyes blaze with a ferocity that speaks of scorched wastelands, a burning testament to their otherworldly origin.

The Falak move as one and then release a tempest of flames that threaten to ensnare those who would stand against them. Hakim and Zenobia are in the firing line, and it's almost impossible to escape the intensity of an otherworldly heat that has the power to singe the very air itself.

The Falak, although mighty, had not reckoned on the mettle of those who stand against them. Hakim's determination is as relentless as the desert winds, and together, he and Zenobia fight as one, two souls bound by courage. Neither will yield to despair. They are the last line of defense against the Vizier's dragoons, and they will stand resolute, come what may.

As a vortex of flame spirals towards them, Hakim's reaction is to call upon the power of the elemental winds. They appear immediately and obey their master, swirling around like a cyclonic gale. And in a split second, the flames of the Falak turn back upon themselves and spare these fearless warriors from a fiery demise.

Zenobia transforms herself into an avian version of a hellfire bird, a creature of such a size that it almost blocks out the sun. But this is no creature from the depths of hell; this is a rainbird. Its massive wings beat ferociously against the heated air, its feathers summoning the water from as far away as the Arabian Sea. And it's not long before the heavens open and a deluge descends upon the blistering forms of the Falak, and when fire meets water, steam is the result.

A torrential downpour quenches their ardour and their fiery power, and within moments, the Falak simply evaporate, their attack thwarted by their nemesis, one of the most powerful elements of the natural world.

"That could have been worse, but it was a clever move on your part. Well done, Zenobia," Hakim says.

"We respond with steel and sorcery and with hearts full of hope."

"We do indeed, and now it's time to go, Aggrabad calls for its defenders."

Despite their tiredness, they venture across the undulating desert sands. Their destination is now within sight, the limestone walls of the Atlantis of the Desert, their home.

As the sun descends below the horizon, casting long shadows across the golden sands, Hakim is surprised to see a small battalion of warriors on the rise of a distant dune.

'We set out in the hope of finding our Captain," one of the men says. The city has suffered a far more significant blow. An earthquake has all but destroyed our home."

"Nature can be a cruel mistress," Hakim says. "She has the power to give, but she also has the power to destroy the little things that we create."

"Even so, you are a very welcome sight," he says joyously. "I wish I could say that your news is heartening but it's not."

He greets his men, all of whom are united, not just by duty, but by a profound connection to the city that has nurtured them.

"Aggrabad now depends on our courage," Hakim says. "The next few days will bring new challenges for our beloved city."

And so, as twilight envelops the desert, Hakim, Zenobia, and a weary band of heroes draw strength from the earth beneath their feet. The natural world whispers a promise of aid to those who seek to preserve its balance. And with each star that appears in the sky, their determination is kindled anew, a flame that will guide them through the perils ahead.

"Aggrabad shall endure, as shall we," Hakim says as they sit around a campfire, his gaze fixed on the silhouette of the city they have vowed to save. "For we are its guardians, and our will is as indomitable as the desert itself."

With the embrace of the cool night air, the company settles into a vigilant rest, their bond with the land and with each other an unbreakable chain.

The wind will carry their silent oaths to every corner of the Rub-al-Khali, to every grain of sand and whispering palm tree. Aggrabad will stand, for its champions have been tempered in the fire of myth and have emerged as legends in their own right.

CHAPTER 13

Dust chokes the air as they reach the crest of a dune that offers a breathtaking view of Aggrabad, but it is a heart-wrenching spectacle of devastation. The ground beneath their feet betrayed the city with tremors, a malignant pulse that sent fractures through its ancient limestone walls.

Buildings that have stood for centuries surrendered to the will of an angry Earth. Proud spires crumbled and walls that once shimmered like a mirage under the desert sun now lay in broken lumps.

"By the ancients," Hakim cries, his voice a low growl of disbelief as he tries to take in the calamity. His piercing green eyes, usually a wellspring of calm authority, now reflect a storm of fear and determination.

"Look at our city," Zenobia cries, horrified by what she sees.

"Stay focused, Zenobia. We have work to do," Hakim says.

He turns to address the loyal guards who respect their captain, but now they will all have to confront the result of the earth's wrath.

"We must form teams and get to work and see what we can do," Hakim says. "People are our priority. Check every crevice and every chamber."

His determination rallies his men into action. They are trained warriors, each of whom has an elevated sense of purpose in his presence.

As the guards disperse, the earth gives another violent shudder, testing the mettle of even the bravest souls. Hakim assesses the situation with the acumen of a seasoned tactician.

"Zenobia," he says. "Take to the air and be our eyes in this our time of need."

"I will search every alcove and every shadow," she says.

Hakim steps hesitantly into the fray, over broken homes and broken lives, hoping to salvage anyone at all from the ruins of despair.

Zenobia circles the sky as a conduit between heaven and earth. Her avian vision pierces the wreckage below, seeking life amidst the rubble. A flutter of movement here, a faint cry there, each a sign of life, a precious spark in the overwhelming gloom.

"There are three survivors on the southeast terrace," she says as she descends.

Hakim moves fast, accompanied by a few of his guards, but it's all too much to take in. The city is like a beast in the final stage of its death throes.

This is treacherous ground, and the earth could swallow them up in a moment, but they have to keep going, and respond when the cries for help grow louder.

They find a family trapped beneath a fallen archway, their eyes wide with terror. It's a distressing sight and nothing short of heartbreaking.

"Peace, we are here to aid you," Hakim says as he cuts through the panic. His presence alone seems to still their minds; his calmness is infectious.

"Captain Al-Rashid," a young handmaiden cries. "Help us, please?"

"Steady now," he says as he extends a hand to lift her out of the debris. "You will survive."

His guards spring into action, carefully shifting the rubble with a strength honed by years of service. One by one, the inhabitants are freed, their expressions morphing from despair to awe as they look upon their rescuers.

"Stay close," Hakim says as he shepherds them to safety." His words are a lifeline in a tumultuous sea of uncertainty.

In the sky above, Zenobia continues her vigilant watch and relays the locations of other trapped souls, her voice the thread that sews the fabric of their survival efforts together.

With every soul they save, Hakim's heart swells with purpose, but the very stones of Aggrabad are crying out in agony. He will not let the city's legacy crumble into nothingness, not if he can do anything about it.

His heart is pounding in his ears, each heartbeat like a war drum as he surges through the wreckage, but every so often, a tremor sends another piece of the city tumbling to its knees, but Hakim is not about to give up.

"Search every shadowy corner. No one is to be left behind." His guards, loyal shadows cast from his own valor are already on the job, and move through the debris with solemn determination, swift and purposeful.

"I have found another family," a guard cries. Hakim hastens to help, only to discover that this is the home of his aunt and uncle, their disbelieving eyes thankful to see a familiar face.

The earth beneath them groans again, but they stand their ground and hope for the best. With disciplined urgency, he and his men move huge chunks of stone without even thinking about it, their muscles straining against the weight.

Sweat mingles with the grime on their skin, but their determination never wavers. They work in unison, guided by the rhythm of Hakim's presence as they move from one shattered home to another.

The floor of one home releases an ominous groan, a warning that its integrity has been compromised. Hakim steps forward to see if anyone has survived, and checks the territory with vigilant eyes.

"Mind your step," he says as he ventures into treacherous ground. "Stay light on your feet."

"Remember, we must save lives," he says. "Focus on the living. We will mourn the dead when time will allow us to do so."

As if in response to his words, a portion of the ceiling crumbles, sending down a shower of smaller stones. Instinctively, the guards form a protective dome with their shields, safeguarding their Captain and themselves from the onslaught.

"Thank you," Hakim says as he acknowledges their swift action. It wasn't just their skill that kept them alive; it was their unity, their willingness to put the safety of others before their own.

"Captain, more people need help," one of the guards says, his voice steady despite the tremors that shake the very air they breathe.

"Then let us press on," Hakim says.

With each step, he becomes more than just their captain, he is the emblem of their survival, the beacon that guides them through the darkness.

They press on even further, following the cries of those trapped beneath fallen walls. Each plea for help fuels their pace, their determination driven by the single purpose of deliverance.

The day wears on and they are still finding people. Sometimes, it's a group of servants from the palace, sometimes a mother and her children, but they are doing their best to battle the rising tide of destruction.

Zenobia is ever vigilant and steers Hakim and his men onto the next horrifying discovery.

"Captain, beware of the east wing. It teeters on the edge of collapse."

The guards step back as the imperiled archway groans ominously, and then take a collective breath when it doesn't do anything other than sway slightly from left to right.

They venture deeper into crumbling corridors, only to discover even more people holding on for dear life.

"Stay on task," he cries to his men, though the command is as much a reminder to himself.

"Captain Al-Rashid," Zenobia cries. "I have found a path into the dungeons, but haste is needed; the foundations weaken by the moment."

"Lead us there, Zenobia," he replies, his trust in her as unyielding as a mountain rock.

And so, they follow the tiny bird that darts with movements swift and sure. Hakim is attuned to the danger that lurks in every crumbling stone and splintered beam. His guards mirror his caution, their eyes scanning constantly, ready to defend or dig through the rubble.

As they approach the gaping entrance to the dungeon, a deep, visceral fear claws at Hakim's chest. It is not dread alone that drives him forward; it is love. It's an inferno that rages against the cold grip of despair, and one that propels him into the bowels of the earth to reclaim whoever may still be alive.

"Be ready for anything," he says, as he draws his sword and steps into the unknown, resolute to the end.

The air in the dungeon is thick with dust and the stench of fear. Torchlights flicker against the walls, casting elongated shadows that dance like demons on the ancient stone. Hakim's grip tightens around his sword as he leads his guards down the final corridor, their boots silent upon the floor.

They arrived at a heavy iron door, barred from within. The muffled sounds of distress seep through the wood, igniting a fire within his chest. With a nod to his men, they brace themselves, knowing that what lies beyond may require the full measure of their valor.

"Cut that door to pieces," Hakim says, his voice a low growl of contained fury.

The guards swing away with their weapons, metal clanging against metal until the barrier gives way with a groan. They surge forward into a dimly lit chamber, only to be met by the Vizier's loyal guards.

"Protect the prisoners," the enemy cries as swords clash in a violent symphony.

Hakim moves with precision, his blade an extension of his will. Each strike is a promise, each parry a testament to his resolve. His men fight with equal ferocity, trained by Hakim himself to be instruments of justice in this lawless hour. They are a whirlwind of steel, muscle, and unwavering determination.

The battle is relentless, each fallen adversary giving rise to yet another struggle, but Hakim will not relent; their honor is a shield against the tide of treachery.

As the last of the Vizier's guards crumble to the ground, the chamber falls quiet, save for the ragged breaths of the victors. Hakim wastes no time, his eyes search the dank cells until they find what they are looking for.

He opens the doors of the cell, only to see half-starved creatures, long marred by despair, but they have come too late. Most have been crushed by the weight of falling masonry, but then, the earth rumbles once again.

"Quickly, we must leave this place," Hakim cries, his voice steady despite the heartbreak that rages within.

With firm resolve, he guides his men to the uncertain light of freedom, each step leading them away from the darkness to whatever else this day may bring.

They stagger through disintegrating halls, each step a thunderous echo in the cacophony of ruin, their muscles tense against the quaking earth beneath their feet. Dust billows like a desert sandstorm, enveloping each of them in a suffocating cloud as they make for the outer world.

"Captain, it looks as if we have trouble on our hands," says one of his men when he sees a familiar figure emerging from the dust.

The Vizier stands before them, resplendent even amidst destruction. Untouched by debris, his robes flow around him like the shadow of a dark sun. He smiles, his lips curling with venomous delight at the sight of Hakim.

"Ah, the noble Captain Al-Rashid, playing hero once more," he says tauntingly, his voice a serpentine hiss that slithers through the air. "You may think you have won, but Aggrabad's end is just the beginning, my dear Hakim."

Hakim instinctively reaches for his sword, the metal singing softly as it begs for release. His eyes, like two emerald flames, lock onto the Vizier.

"Your quarrel is with me, not with innocent people," Hakim says as diplomatically as he can. The desire for vengeance tugs at his heartstrings. He loosens the grip on his sword; this is not the moment of reckoning; there are lives to be saved and futures to secure.

"Remember your duty," says a quiet voice within.

"We have work to do," Hakim says. "We have people to save."

"Such touching concern," the Vizier says. "Flee then, you coward. Run with your tail between your legs. Know that wherever you go, my wrath shall follow."

Hakim pauses, a part of him yearning to silence the Vizier's poisonous words forever. Yet, with a deep breath, he steels his heart and is about to leave, but the Vizier is not finished yet.

"Evacuating your rats from a sinking ship, Captain," the Vizier says as his low and menacing voice slithers through the air, and tinges the unsettled silence with malice. His eyes glint, and reflect the light with eerie luminosity.

"Every soul deserves to be safe," Hakim says as he plants himself firmly between the evacuees and the looming threat. "We will leave Aggrabad to your twisted desires."

Memphalut's lips curl into a contemptuous sneer. "Noble sentiments for a man who is watching his world crumble. Tell me, Captain, how do you plan to save your beloved city when its foundations turn to ash? How many lives will weigh on your conscience?"

"Mockery is the tool of the powerless," Hakim retorts, his gaze unwavering. "Your words hold no sway here."

"Powerless, are you," The Dark Conjurer laughs, a cold sound that resonates through the fractured city. "You have yet to see my true strength."

Hakim is aware of a power deep within his soul, but the weight of responsibility anchors his spirit. He knows the sort of torment that the Vizier could unleash, but fear has no dominion over his duty.

"Your reign ends tonight, Vizier. Aggrabad will be free of your darkness."

Everyone is watching closely, their concern rising like the heat of the desert wind. They believe in Hakim and have faith that he will stand unyielding, the last shield of innocence before tyranny.

"Let us hope for your sake that you are right," the Vizier says as he raises his staff high, the crystal skull at the apex catching the firelight with a sinister glow.

"Hope is but a companion, Vizier," Hakim says, his hand resting on the hilt of his scimitar. "It is courage that carves the path to victory."

The grand hall of Aggrabad's palace, once a testament to its beauty and craftsmanship, now bears the scars of impending doom. Amidst its majestic pillars and the remnants of its opulent decor, two figures stand opposed, the fate of an entire city in their hands.

To the vizier's surprise, Hakim raises his arms, and a stream of blinding light surges from his fingertips, and their target is the master of evil, Memphalut al Shikari.

The Vizier responds immediately and raises his staff into the air to absorb the electric assault before it can do any damage.

"Your newfound tricks are infantile, Captain," he cries, his voice dripping with contempt as he thrusts his staff into the air once again.

From the depths of the shadows, the grotesque forms of Nasnas appear, snarling beasts under the command of the Vizier. Their target is Hakim; their vicious limbs are outstretched, and their sharp claws seek flesh.

Hakim has a past that the Vizier is not aware of. In his youthful days, he was trained by a long-gone sorcerer to remember incantations, words of power whispered into his mind.

Those words were never forgotten, and at that moment, he releases a cascade of cosmic power and repels the Nasnas with a force that sends them back to the abyss from whence they came.

"Your creatures cower, Vizier," Hakim declares, his voice resounding through the fractured hall. He raises his hands, his palms glowing with burgeoning might, and unleashes a volley of flaming orbs. They shoot through the air, trailing sparks and smoke as they seek their dark-cloaked target.

Memphalut deflects them with swift, precise movements, but as the barrage continues, he is forced to conjure a series of spectral shields, each one disintegrating under the relentless onslaught.

With a snarl of frustration, he retaliates, chanting words that seem to scrape against the very fabric of reality. From the gnarled tip of his staff, tendrils of shadow burst forth, heading for Hakim. They twist and turn and seek to ensnare him in their choking grasp, but Hakim moves with the grace of the desert wind and responds with a spell of his own.

A pool of water forms beneath the Vizier's feet and threatens to encase him in a block of solid ice, but he recoils and stands firm. Undeterred, he reaches deep into his well of sorcery, his eyes gleaming with malignant intensity.

He summons the Falak, the serpent demons of legend from their infernal realm and commands them to do his will. With their scales glinting like liquid fire, they slither into existence, their very presence distorting the air around.

"Face me without your minions," Hakim bellows. Before they can strike, he manifests a blade of power out of thin air, and the Vizier's evil army dissolves into smoldering wisps upon contact with the enchanted steel.

A clash of light and dark, of courage and malice, rages within the heart of Aggrabad, as protector and usurper weave a tapestry of destruction and defiance with every spell they cast and parry.

"This must end," Hakim cries.

The Vizier is relentless and attempts to conjure up yet another barrage of arcane missiles, but Hakim counteracts them the curse before it has even left his lips.

"Your efforts are futile, Hakim," the Vizier sneers with a predatory grin as he prepares to conjure up yet another destructive force.

Hakim has had enough of this charade and summons a wall of whirling sand to deflect the Vizier's attack. Then, seizing the moment, he lunges at the Vizier with the force of his will, but the Vizier deflects the blade with uncanny speed.

His silhouette, stark against the flickering torchlight, the Vizier's control is waning. With a flourish of his staff, he seeks to ensnare Hakim in a web of dark enchantment.

"Thou shall not escape, Captain," he cries, the venom in his voice almost tangible. "The abyss calls to thee."

His muscles are tense, and the oppressive weight of the Vizier's spell threaten to crush Hakim's will, but in his veins runs the legacy of his forebears, warriors all, a lineage that will not yield to tyranny.

Drawing from a wellspring of fortitude deep within his soul, Hakim conjures up an ancient incantation passed down through many generations.

The shadows recoil as if scorched by invisible flames, and the web unravels before his indomitable spirit. Seizing a momentary reprieve, he extends his hands, palms outstretched towards the malevolent conjurer. And from somewhere deep within, a powerful energy surges forth, a cascading torrent of radiant light that roars like the wind in a tempest.

The sound of his voice shatters the walls of the palace, and it's very foundations groan under the strain. The air crackles with a primal energy, an explosive sound that echoes far and wide.

Hakim is not about to allow the Dark Conjurer to survive for a moment longer. "Your days of cruelty are over," he cries.

As the palace crumbles into dust, the Vizier realises that this could mean the end. A moment later, the earth moves again and the ground parts, and he realises that he is stranded on a narrow ledge and balancing precariously on the edge of an abyss.

"Your city falls, Captain, and with it, your hope," the Vizier cries, but Hakim is undeterred. His eyes are alive with fierce resolve.

"Aggrabad will endure in its people, and I am their shield," Hakim cries back.

He stops for a moment and takes a breath, all too aware that this confrontation is being watched by over a thousand desperate and horrified citizens. They are his heart, his purpose, the very soul of Aggrabad, and for them, he is about to unleash the full might of his power.

He summons his ancestral spirits, warriors who have defended this land since time immemorial. He bids them to stand at his side and lend strength to his weary campaign.

"By the eternal sands, I banish you to hellfire," he cries, and at that moment, a torrent of powerful cosmic energy erupts from his very core. It swirls around in a vortex of heat and brilliance and coalesces into a blinding spear, its tip crackling with the raw fury of a desert storm.

And on Hakim's command, a light of pure power and intensity pierces the dark heart of the Vizier, and in a rare moment of fear, Memphalut's eyes widen as he realises that this is the end.

As the vibrating spear heads for its target, those watching these events from the sidelines hold their breath, and wait for justice to be served once and for all.

What follows is like a blizzard of incandescent fury that leaves no shadow untouched. Memphalut al Shikari, once a figure of dread and power, is caught in a tempest of his own design. And before he has an opportunity to release yet another incantation, his body explodes like a desert storm.

"Your malice ends here," Hakim cries as he drops to his knees.

It is then that the palace groans and crumbles to the ground. The ground trembles violently, sending fractures racing across the surface like lightning. With a deafening crack, it opens wide, and the remains of the Vizier disappear into an abyss created by his own wicked schemes.

For a fleeting moment, time seems to stand still, and before Hakim disappears over the edge of a bottomless ravine, Zenobia comes to his rescue.

She soars down on a graceful wind, a majestic eagle descending from the smoke-filled sky. Her golden plumage glints with flashes of light, a beacon of hope amidst the darkness. She circles once, her keen eyes assesses the situation, and then swoops down and raises Hakim into the air with her massive claws and places him on the very edge of the battlefield.

Zenobia reverts to her human form and takes him in her arms, but something is wrong; Hakim is no longer there. And then, a few moments later, his chest heaves, his breath returns, and Zenobia sighs with relief.

"Thank you," he says as he gazes into her loving eyes. She just nods but her heart is beating so fast that she can barely even speak,

Around them, the once grand city of Aggrabad lies cloaked in devastation, its buildings fractured and silhouetted against a sky now streaked with dawn's first light. The scent of jasmine that once perfumed the streets is no longer there, nothing but the stench of scorched stone and despair.

"Look at the devastation he has wrought," Hakim sighs, his voice filled with pain for the loss of the city he loves, now reduced to nothing but rubble.

Zenobia places a comforting hand on his arm; her touch is light but firm. "This is not the end, Hakim. Aggrabad shall rise from the ashes."

His eyes meet hers, and he finds solace in her unwavering spirit.

"Aye, we will rebuild, stronger and more united than ever before. This is but the dawn of a new era," he says as he gestures towards the horizon.

"Then let us begin," Zenobia says, her voice steady with resolution. "Aggrabad will need its guardians. We will stand by our people, protect and guide them, and help them build a new home."

"And so it shall be," he says.

"Our journey continues, and though the path may be fraught with perils unknown, we will face them together."

The survivors of this catastrophe are huddled together, looking very lost. Most of them are shell-shocked, dazed, and weary, but they are alive.

Hakim and Zenobia stand shoulder to shoulder, ready to lead and inspire. They share a silent promise to nurture the seeds of revival sown by their resilience, setting the stage for whatever awaits them in the world out there.

As they pass through the remnants of the city gates, the vast expanse of the unforgiving desert is the only thing that greets them. They dare not look back as Aggrabad surrenders to its fate, but before them lies the promise of another future, and it is waiting for anyone daring enough to redefine their destiny.

Hakim pauses and allows himself one final look back at the city that gave him a purpose in life. Then, with the resolute stride of a leader born and bred for such times, he leads his flock into the wilderness.

"To the dunes," he cries, his voice as steady as the ancient mountains. "Our story is not yet finished."

Accompanied by his guards, they lead several thousand people into the unknown, each step a testament to their resolve. They will be the guardians of Aggrabad's legacy, the keeper of its tales, and the architects of whatever is yet to come.

A soft wind stirs the desert sands, whispering promises of renewal to the weary survivors who follow along behind. Hakim is constantly scanning the horizon, where the relentless sun heralds the end of one chapter and the beginning of another.

In her human form, Zenobia walks with purpose beside the man she loves, her gaze sweeping over the remnants of Aggrabad. The once dazzling white limestone is now dulled by ash and dust, but it is not beyond salvation. Her fingers brush against the hilt of her sword, a small gesture that grounds her in the reality of the task ahead.

The faces of the survivors are etched with sorrow for what they have lost, yet alight with an indomitable spirit that even the Vizier's malice could not extinguish.

"They look to us for guidance," Hakim says.

"And guide them we shall," Zenobia replies, the melodic cadence of her voice bolsters his resolve. She pauses to help a young boy disentangle his clothing from a jagged piece of metal and offers him a smile that belies the fatigue clinging to her bones.

Hakim watches her with admiration. In the face of destruction, she is a beacon of compassion and strength. "As guardians of this city, our duty remains clear," he says, his words carrying the weight of responsibility.

"Indeed," Zenobia responds, "but it will take time, patience, and the combined will of every beating heart."

"Aggrabad will rise once again," she says, Her eyes capturing the first light of dawn.

They are pilgrims on a mission and have no idea where they are going. Children cling to the skirts of their mothers, while hardened warriors tend quietly to their wounds, all under the watchful eye of their leaders, Hakim and Zenobia.

"We must ensure that everyone has water and shelter," Hakim says, his deep voice cutting through the desolation like a clarion call. "We will rebuild, not just buildings but hope as well."

"Hope is our most potent magic," Zenobia says, her presence a comfort to the unsettled crowd. She raises her arms and addresses the people of Aggrabad with unwavering confidence. "From the ruins, we will forge our future. Together, there is nothing we cannot accomplish."

A cheer rises from the multitude, a sound tinged with both pain and triumph. As the survivors rally around their shared vision, the Captain of the Guards knows that the true measure of their strength lies not in the might of their walls but in their resilience as a community.

As the last echoes of Zenobia's speech mingle with the wind, they stand side by side, faces set against the dawning day. They have faced the darkness together, and now, amidst the rubble of their fallen city, they will build a bastion of light.

They join hands and make a silent oath, a vow to protect, to rebuild, and to lead the people of Aggrabad into an era of prosperity undreamt of before. I will be a new dawn for the people of the Atlantis of the Desert, and Hakim and Zenobia will be its harbingers.

CHAPTER 14

Like rain drops in the desert sun, their hearts now lay in ruins, littering the landscape with emotional debris and the ghosts of splendor lost. They have no choice but to navigate the dunes with steadfast purpose, scanning the horizon for hope amidst the tumult.

"Stay close and shield the young ones," says the ever-vigilant Hakim.

Zenobia moves with graceful purpose, her dark hair billowing like a banner of hope against the backdrop of destruction. They are an unlikely pair: he was born to a lineage of warriors with an arcane heritage, and she was the daughter of a bird seller who was granted the power of transformation by the very same old sorcerer. Together, they are bound, and not just by love but by unseen cosmic forces.

"There is a gorge in those mountains up ahead," Hakim says. "There could be water in those hills."

A mother clutching an infant stumbles and falls, and with reflexes honed by years of battle, Hakim helps her up and takes the infant in his arms.

"Captain, the gorge seems to be blocked by stones on the western side," a guard says as he returns, breathless from sprinting through the labyrinth.

"Then we will pass through the eastern side," he says. "Zenobia, make sure that the rear flank keeps pace. We leave no soul behind."

"Understood," she says as she weaves her way among the evacuees, offering words of comfort and firm encouragement.

As she surveys those who survived, Zenobia's deep brown eyes move from face to face with hawkish intensity. Her heart aches for these people, their lives uprooted in an instant, but she knows despair will serve no one.

She clasps the amulet around her neck, a talisman that pulses with ancient energy, and a moment later, she soars on powerful wings to take a closer look at the path ahead.

The landscape beyond the gorge is endless miles of undulating dunes that may hold danger, but hopefully, it will also be a promise of refuge. Zenobia watches from above, her heart is with each and every person on this journey, and she is as much a guardian of their spirits as she is a sentinel against the perils of the journey.

They press on wearily, the desert sun beating down upon them with unrelenting fervor as if it seeks to claim its due. Even though his throat burns with thirst, Hakim's focus never wavers, each step a silent vow to lead his people to safety.

The sand is their enemy and is as relentless as any storm stirred up by the chaos they have left behind. Some people are all but ready to give up as they trudge through the scorching desert sand.

"Don't stop, please. We have to keep moving," Hakim cries, his voice hoarse with thirst and worry. He digs deep to find the energy to rally the spirits of those who follow along behind, and then the impossible happens.

"Water," Zenobia cries. "There's an oasis not far from here."

"Then lead us to it," Hakim says, "before we all die of thirst."

With each step they take, their muscles are screaming, rebelling against the relentless exertion. Even the guards trudging alongside of civilians are dying of fatigue. The weight of their swords has never felt so burdensome, but the responsibility they symbolise has never been so vital.

"Stay strong," Hakim cries and then murmurs a silent prayer, as much for himself as it is for others. It's a silent plea to his ancestors, those who walked these lands in the days of old, warriors of renown who faced their own trials with bravery.

As the day wanes, the shadows lengthen, and by the time they reach the oasis, everyone is moving on instinct, their minds a million miles away, occupied with thoughts in distant places.

As night descends upon an oasis in the desert, a cool breeze whispers across the vast expanse and calls to each and every one of them.

"Guide us, please," Hakim says, as he whispers a silent prayer to his celestial guardians. "Protect my people and my family until we reach safer shores."

Their journey is not over yet, but they carry on under the Sun's determined glare and the Moon's watchful eye. Despite their exhaustion, they press on, driven by Hakim's indomitable will and the promise of salvation that lay beyond the dunes.

"Rest will come soon," he assures them, even though his limbs tremble with the effort as every fiber of his being is pushed to its limit.

The next morning, the first hint of dawn casts a pale light over the weary band of survivors, and Hakim's eyes scan the horizon in the hope of salvation.

Amidst the lingering fears, a subtle strength emerges, binding them together like the woven fabric of a Bedouin tent, resilient and steadfast.

Hakim feels a swell of pride for these people, and even though they have lost everything, they still have the capacity to keep going.

"Lean on me, brother," one man says to another. His strength has waned, so he drapes his arms around his comrade's shoulder.

"Here, take my scarf, it will shield your child from the sand," a woman says as she unwinds the cloth from her head and places it gently over an infant cradled in its mother's arms.

"See, Zenobia," Hakim says. "Even in the darkest of times, hope flickers like a flame in the wind."

Zenobia smiles, her gaze reflecting the light of that very hope. "It is more than a flicker, Hakim. It is the fire that warms our spirits and guides us through the night."

The journey stretches on, the sun climbs higher in the sky and bakes the sand beneath their feet. Yet, with each step they take, the sound of the sea beckons, a siren's call that promises respite and renewal.

And then, one morning, they wake up, and their senses are assailed by a familiar salty smell wafting through the air. To the few who have ventured beyond Aggrabad, they recognise it as the aroma of the ocean.

A few hours later, they see the coastline for the very first time. A collective gasp ripples through the crowd as the vast expanse of the Arabian Sea reveals itself to one and all, the water glimmering like a mirage made real. The air carries the scent of salt and freedom and mingles with the dry spice of the desert they have left behind.

"Look upon the sea, my friends," Hakim cries, as his voice cries clear and strong. "Let that sight wash away your weariness. We have endured the wrath of the desert, and now it gifts us passage to a new beginning."

A cheer erupts from parched lips, eyes brimming, not with tears of sorrow, but with relief and joy. Together, they have traversed the unforgiving sands, a caravan of lost and forsaken souls, all of whom are bound by shared trials and triumphs.

"Behold, the gateway to our future," Zenobia cries, "and look upon a horizon of possibilities as yet unseen."

As they approach the point where the golden sand meets the embrace of the turquoise waves, Hakim allows himself to believe in the promise of the tales of old, about ships returning from other lands rich with opportunity and peace.

"Aggrabad lives on within us," he proclaims, his heart echoing with the rhythm of the tides. "Our journey is not finished yet, it begins anew this day, upon these shores."

With the vastness of the ocean spread out before them, Hakim and Zenobia stand side by side, their resolve mirrored in the faces of those who fled from the ruin and into the arms of hope's gentle shore.

As Hakim peers into the vastness, the salt-tinged breeze whispers of distant lands. And then, as if summoned by their collective longing, the silhouettes of long graceful ships appear on the horizon, and move towards the shore like a flock of seagulls converging upon a hidden treasure.

"Zenobia, do you see?" Hakim cries. His voice wavers with emotion as he points at a flotilla of ships dancing upon the water.

She transforms once again and soars up into the sky, the shadow of the great Roc sweeping over the ocean. A jubilant cry escapes her beak, a sound that transcends human speech as she circles above, confirming the sight they have longed to see.

She descends and resumes her human form, her eyes ablaze with excitement. "Boats from lands unknown, carrying promises of tomorrow."

The survivors cluster around, murmurs of disbelief turning to gasps of amazement. Even the most stoic among them let slip smiles of wonder, their gaze latching onto the vessels that grow more distinct with each passing moment.

"Could it be traders or explorers from afar?" a young man says, hope threading through his words like golden strands.

"Whoever they are, they bring the winds of change," Hakim replies, his heart pounding in rhythm with the waves lapping at the shore.

It is then that one dhow captures their attention, its sails a striking crimson that blazes against the azure canvas of the sky and the sea. It cuts through the water with a majesty that commands the very ocean to make way.

At the prow stands a figure both grand and enigmatic, draped in robes of deep blue embroidered with threads of silver and gold. Even though the distance obscures the finer details, there is an unmistakable air of adventure that clings to this man like the sea spray on the vessel's bow.

"By the heavens," Hakim cries, transfixed by what he sees. "It's Sinbad.".

"Could it truly be?" Zenobia says as she leans closer to seek confirmation of his claim.

"Legends often hold truth nestled within their folds," Hakim says, his voice steady despite the thrumming of his heart. "And perhaps, we are to be part of a new legend, one that begins today."

The red-sailed dhow draws near enough for the survivors to discern the radiant smile of the captain, and a sense of anticipation grips them all. His demeanor speaks of thrilling escapades across untamed seas and treasures plucked from the grip of perilous quests.

"Prepare yourselves, my friends," Hakim says as he rallies the weary but spirited throng. "A new chapter awaits us, an odyssey, not of escape, but of discovery."

The setting sun casts a fiery glow upon the scene, but the dhow's majestic silhouette promises a future laden with mystery and the allure of the unknown. When the ship finally reaches shallow water, it drops anchor, and every heart on the beach pulsates with the promise of adventures yet to come.

This is not the immortal Sinbad, but it doesn't really matter. He is a saviour and he is gracious enough to offer them the opportunity of a lifetime.

"Come with us and sail the Seven Seas, and we will find a place that you can call home. What do you say to that?" the Captain says.

'We have nowhere else to go, and we gratefully accept that offer," Hakim says.

The gangplanks of each and every ship are lowered with a resonant thud and everyone prepares for the adventure of a lifetime. The boundless horizon mingled with the murmur of anticipation calls. Zenobia stands by Hakim's side, her eyes reflecting the golden tapestry of sky and water where the sun meets the sea in a final fiery embrace.

"We are about to go somewhere and do something we have never done before," Hakim says, his voice now rich with hope. "Are you ready?"

"More than I have ever been," Zenobia replies. "This is not the end, but a new beginning."

One by one, the survivors move hesitantly up the gangplanks of each ship, their faces etched with stories of loss and resilience. Hakim reaches out, clasping hands, offering nods of encouragement. Zenobia, ever the beacon, smiles warmly, her presence a soothing balm to the frayed spirits.

A young boy called Abu, who is no more than ten summers old, tugs at Hakim's tunic.

"Captain," he says, his voice barely above a whisper. "Are there monsters out there?"

Hakim gets down on his knees and places a firm hand on his shoulder. "Abu, there are probably quite a few monsters in those waters out there, but they won't bother us.'

'Be not concerned as there will always be monsters of one kind or another. But we will face them together because we are warriors of the light, and that is our power, and it always has been."

The boy nods, his eyes alight with newfound determination, and then runs off and joins the people heading for the dhow. Hakim rises to his feet, and his heart swells with pride for these people who have lost everything yet refuse to be broken.

"Behold," Zenobia, he says as he gestures toward the horizon, "the path ahead may be veiled in mystery, but it is ours to chart."

Together, they ascend the gangplank, each step a silent vow to forge a destiny worthy of legend. The planks creak beneath their feet and the rhythm of adventure calls from the deep. The crew hasten about, securing ropes and unfurling the majestic red sails that billow like the wings of a phoenix rising from the ashes.

"Set sail," the captain cries as his voice carries across the waves.

The dhow surges forward and cuts through the water with purpose and grace. Hakim takes one last look at the coastline as it recedes into the distance. No longer is it a boundary but a memory, a testament to survival and spirit.

"Zenobia, whatever lies ahead, I am glad to face it with you." Their fingers intertwine, a symbol of their woven destinies. "Together," she says, "we are unstoppable."

As the dhow ventures into the open sea, the stars emerge as ancient sentinels lighting their passage. The survivors huddle close, their whispers and songs crafting a tapestry of unity and shared dreams.

Hakim guided them to freedom with a steady hand, his resolve as unyielding as the rock that withstands a relentless tide. And Zenobia, her eyes set on the vast expanse that lies before them, sees not the darkness of uncertainty but a canvas awaiting the bold strokes of those daring enough to dream.

The dhow sails ever onwards, a silhouette against a celestial map, a symbol of their indomitable will, as they sail toward a future rife with untold possibilities. As the last light of day surrenders to the symphony of night, Hakim and Zenobia stand at the prow, ready to embrace the odyssey that beckons with the promise of a new dawn.

THE END

The Gods of Space and Time
A SERIES OF FANTASY FICTION STORIES

The Gods of Space and Time are a series of fantasy fiction stories and epic adventures and they all have one thing in common. They are based on the belief that people are the most important things in life, not possessions or power or knowledge, but people.

The characters are died-in-the-wool humanitarians, and when they do encounter violence, they deal with it using creative non-violent methods.

These books have a host of wonderful characters, great dialogue, humour, of course, and that most indispensable of all qualities... heart and soul.

You have probably noticed that just about every modern day movie and just as many books are about subjecting people to violence in one form or another.

I have no interest in perpetuating that ideology in any way at all, or indeed of subjecting my characters to that form of thinking. In my mind, violence is not and never has been a form of entertainment.

Unlike his brother who is cautious and irritable, Addric has a bit of a reputation. He not only believes in miracles; he also believes in the impossible.

Their holiday plans are sabotaged from the first day and they barely survive one life threatening situation after another. The stakes are high and they have to succeed.

A card-carrying member of the dark side is out to get his revenge, but they can't allow that to happen. Addric rises to the challenge and shows what he is made of.

He proves to everyone that he is both brilliant, and audacious. Fearless is a rollercoaster ride through an inter-dimensional realm, a place where unusual things can happen.

A drama set in motion long, long ago is about to unfold. All they wanted was a boy's own holiday. They had no idea what sort of holiday they were in for.

THE OCEAN OF INFINITE MYSTERY

Allow your mind to roam further than it has ever done before, to the outer perimeter of Alpha Centauri. It is here you will find a galaxy called the Khavala, an inter-dimensional realm, where many worlds exist side-by-side, a world of strange beauty, hidden power, and wondrous mystery.

The Khavala is a self-conscious entity, but when danger threatens the most sacrosanct of all domains, she calls upon the assistance of her most powerful creations, an invincible task force that includes Yumi Masters and Warrior Angels.

To resolve this problem, they must travel deep into the heart centre of the Khavala, to a place of legend, to the domain known since time immemorial as The Ocean of Infinite Mystery.

THE LAST DAYS OF LEMURIA

Elisabeth Trundle's life changes on the day that she meets two young men in The Great Library of London, but these guys are not Earthlings.

Elisabeth has been having dreams about the lost continent of Lemuria ever since she was a child.

But the last thing she expected is that she would actually get an opportunity to go there. And that would never have happened if the chronometer of a passing spaceship had not malfunctioned.

Accompanied by four Yumi Masters, Elisabeth's dream comes true and she ends up in a civilisation that's about to be destroyed by a natural catastrophe. Over the next two weeks, they have to train an army, defeat the high priest at his own game and save a young boy's life.

But it's not all bad news, the people are wonderful and the food is even better. Before the dreaded day dawns, they discover how the Lemurians intend to survive.

Accompanied by a few feisty friends, Addric embarks on a mission to rescue his brother's girlfriend from the clutches of a necromancer with delusions of grandeur.

To save Elisabeth, they will have to battle it out in the Roman arena, cross the Arctic Ocean on a crystal powered boat, venture deep into the bowels of the Earth, and then brave the fires of hell on a volcanic planet on the verge of a major transformation.

It will take something more than sharp claws and attitude to defeat a necromancer at his own game, but these boys are Yumi Masters and they have a few tricks up their sleeve.

SAYONARA PLANET EARTH

It is Tuesday, the 13th of May 2032, and it's almost D-Day, and 80,000 people in St. Peter's Square are awaiting the arrival of a saviour. He appears at the door of a luminous gateway and makes his way down a winding staircase. He has the physique of a Spartan warrior and is dressed in a suit of white leather.

Addric Sharano is about to reveal his true identity to seven billion Earthlings. Addric is an alien, and he is on a mission. The people of Earth have lost touch with the very essence of who and what they are. They have been seduced by the allure of electronic devices. The big guys upstairs are willing to give them one more chance but only if they change their ways.

On that day, Addric became an instant celebrity and he was going to use it to his advantage. There's a time limit on this deal. If the people of Earth want to survive, they have to change their ways. Addric is not about to fail and he is definitely not interested in ever having to say, "Sayonara Planet Earth."

Earth is his home as well.

QUIETLY, THEY CAME

The master of fun and games is back, and Addric is in fine form in this light-hearted adventure. His next mission is to rescue forty-two orphans from Pompeii, before they are incinerated by the volcano.

Accompanied by his best friends and glamorous offsiders, Lady Felicity, and her sister, Demetra, two exponents of the fine old art of subterfuge, and the modern version of sorcery, Addric comes up with a clever if not complicated plan.

However, there is one little catch. These kids have a greater purpose in life. They were born with a coded message in their DNA, and it's just waiting for an opportunity to be expressed.

Addric is not known as the master of spin for nothing, so, he takes them by the hand and they dive into the deep end. And when they come up for air, they hit the big time.

Addric is the man with golden touch, and when it comes to doing the impossible he delivers the goods in this rollicking romp of a story. Sit back and enjoy a ride that starts in Pompeii and ends on some of the great stages of the modern world.

The future of an inconspicuous village is threatened by an ungodly invader, but a prophecy states that a messiah will come to their rescue.

The first person on the scene is a Yumi Master with a history of battling the bad guys. And not long after, the real messiah appears in a blaze of glory. Disposing of the invaders is a serious business, but they have quite a few tricks up their sleeve, and the most potent weapon in their armoury is the power of sound.

And when they are not doing that, they entertain the musically inclined villagers with a selection of inspirational songs from the 20th century.

While some of those have a specific purpose, others are perennial favourites that have no purpose, other than to elevate your vibrational frequency. It's a tough call, but someone has to do it. A story to put a smile on your face.

A PRAYER FOR BROTHER WILLIAM

After he loses his parents, William Cahill, retreats into a world of his own and his life would have spiralled out of control if it had not been for Aunt Augusta.

She drags him back from the brink and transforms his life and that of his siblings, but Augusta Cahill is no ordinary woman.

She might be dreadfully wealthy and a pathetic old socialite, but she can be a force to be reckoned with.

This is a story about life, death and suffering on the home front, a place that can be as perilous as a battlefield.

Based on an old family legend about love letters than never reached their destination.

KASHMIRA
The Snake Charmer's Wife

The Snake Charmer's Wife is a story about an orphan called Govinda who raises his children, Roshan and Kashmira, to become the most celebrated snake charmers of 19th century Ceylon.

After an untimely death, Kashmira embarks on the life of a time-travelling spirit and makes an appearance in the life of Jasper Powell, a young man from modern-day Melbourne. Kashmira has unfinished business and she chooses Jasper and his girlfriend Sally to complete a task that she could not. This book was a finalist in, The 2019 Book Excellence Awards.

ABOUT THE AUTHOR

Vincent Gilvarry is a writer from tropical North Queensland in Australia and one whose creative journey traverses the realms of imagination and of artistic expression.

With a foundation based in the visual arts, his transition into the realm of literature was sparked by a life-changing situation that inspired him to embark on a literary career and an odyssey that has lasted for over 25 years.

He boasts an eclectic repertoire that showcases his versatility across various genres and his fantasy fiction books in particular are a testament to his unparalleled imagination and his narrative prowess.

He is the author of a series of eight fantasy fiction books, a romance novel and a historical fiction based on an old family legend.

Copyright
2024
Vincent Gilvarry
©

9 781763 747616